PRAISE FOR *BEST BABYSITTERS EVER*

"A clever twist on an old favorite, *Best Babysitters Ever* sparkles with humor and attitude. A must-read for the middle school set!"
—MELISSA DE LA CRUZ, #1 *NEW YORK TIMES* BEST-SELLING AUTHOR

"A glitter-dusted story about ambition, revenge, forgiveness, and friendship. Add to cart!"
—LISI HARRISON, *NEW YORK TIMES* BEST-SELLING AUTHOR OF *THE CLIQUE*

"Hilarious, fresh, and fun! *Best Babysitters Ever* is the best! A great homage to a classic series with plenty of modern moxie."
—MICOL OSTOW, BEST-SELLING AUTHOR OF *MEAN GIRLS: A NOVEL*

"From the start of this debut novel, Cala flexes her prodigious comedic muscles, managing to render the three friends both as sympathetic heroines and as the victims of lives more humorous than they would like. . . . They may never get another babysitting gig, but you're hooked on their story for life."
—*NEW YORK TIMES* BOOK REVIEW

"In her middle grade debut, Cala artfully uses humorous banter to paint the dissimilar friends' realistic relationships as well as their bumbling efforts to vocalize their feelings and advocate for themselves. . . . An appealing, humor-filled update to a classic series."
—*PUBLISHERS WEEKLY*

"Thanks to witty banter, ample humor, and excellent characterization, readers will enjoy following this group of young dreamers as they attempt to gain some independence in their preteen lives." **—*KIRKUS REVIEWS***

"A breezy, entertaining read, this book and the promised sequels seem likely to fill a role similar to the original—as reading material kids choose for themselves." **—*HORN BOOK***

"Fans of the Baby-Sitters Club books are a natural fit for this debut novel about three enterprising girls. . . . Cala incorporates themes of sibling rivalry, jealousy, competition, friendship, manipulation, entrepreneurship, and first crushes into this realistic series starter."
—*BOOKLIST*

"Even readers who have never had the pleasure of hanging out with the BC girls of yore will find Malia, Bree, and Dot all likable in their distinct ways, and they'll appreciate the book's mix of snark and heart." **—*THE BULLETIN***

PRAISE FOR *THE GOOD, THE BAD, AND THE BOSSY*

"This smart, humorous tale should inspire girls to dream big, experiment, and problem-solve through challenges." **—*KIRKUS REVIEWS***

"This light, amusing installment features relatable characters who are imperfect yet well meaning." **—*SCHOOL LIBRARY JOUNRAL***

THE GOOD, THE BAD,
AND
THE BOSSY

Best ~~BAD~~ BABYSITTERS Ever

THE GOOD, THE BAD, AND THE BOSSY

CAROLINE CALA

HOUGHTON MIFFLIN HARCOURT

BOSTON   NEW YORK

hmhbooks.com

Produced by Alloy Entertainment

alloy**entertainment**

30 Hudson Yards, 22nd Floor
New York, NY 10001
alloyentertainment.com

The text was set in Garamond.
Cover and interior design by Opal Roengchai

The Library of Congress has cataloged the hardcover edition as follows:
Names: Cala, Caroline, author.
Title: The good, the bad, and the bossy / Caroline Cala.
Description: Boston ; New York : Houghton Mifflin Harcourt , [2019] | Series: Best babysitters ever ; 2 | Summary: When other commitments threaten the success of the Best Babysitters Ever, Malia is frustrated until she comes up with a plan to hire new babysitters and take a cut of their wages. | Identifiers: LCCN 2018051355 (print) | LCCN 2018055226 (ebook) Subjects: | CYAC: Babysitters—Fiction. | Clubs—Fiction. | Moneymaking projects—Fiction. | Best friends—Fiction. | Friendship—Fiction. | Humorous stories. | BISAC: JUVENILE FICTION / Social Issues / Friendship. | JUVENILE FICTION / Humorous Stories. | JUVENILE FICTION / Business, Careers, Occupations. | JUVENILE FICTION / Social Issues / Adolescence. Classification: LCC PZ7.1.C27 (ebook) | LCC PZ7.1.C27 Goo 2019 (print) | DDC [Fic]—dc23
LC record available at https://lccn.loc.gov/2018051355

ISBN: 978-1-328-85090-4 paper over board
ISBN: 978-0-358-54766-2 paperback

Manufactured in the United States of America
1 2021
4500824224

Best ~~BAD~~ BABYSITTERS Ever

THE GOOD, THE BAD,
AND
THE BOSSY

CHAPTER ONE

MALIA

Sometimes, if she tried really hard, Malia Twiggs could remember a time when she thought boogers were gross. It's not that she currently *liked* boogers—she hadn't gotten an entirely new personality or anything—but in the months since starting her own babysitting club, she had definitely learned to make peace with them. It was amazing, really, the limitless boundaries of personal growth.

"Don't worry about a thing!" Malia yelled, waving across the yard to her best friends and fellow babysitters, Bree Robinson and Dot Marino. "I've got this situation under control."

The situation at hand was a crying Jonah Gregory, their four-year-old babysitting charge who had just tripped while chasing a butterfly. The damage seemed to be two skinned knees and a lot of tears but, thankfully, nothing else.

Bree offered a little salute and Dot nodded before they turned their attention back to the other three Gregory children.

Malia calmly guided Jonah across the yard and into the house. As a now-experienced babysitter, she knew exactly how to clean and bandage his scraped knees, tell a goofy joke to put an end to the tears, and, yes, do away with his crying-induced snot.

"BUT IT HUWTS!" yelled Jonah, who could not yet pronounce the *r* sound.

"I know it hurts, but look how brave you are," Malia said, expertly applying a Band-Aid emblazoned with smiling cartoon rabbits. "And now that you're all patched up, I have a surprise for you."

Jonah continued to pout.

"You get to have ice cream!"

At the mention of a frozen treat, Jonah's small, chubby face visibly brightened.

Babysitting had taught Malia many things, including how easily little children could be bribed with snacks, how willing they were to believe whatever an older person told them, and, last but certainly not least, how nice it was to buy things with your own money. But on a deeper level, babysitting had shown her what it meant to transform. One day, you could be a regular seventh-grader with no crisis management skills whatsoever, and then, before you knew it, there you were: herding four children around a home, all while making grilled cheeses, breaking up a fight, and negotiating nap time like it was nothing. For Malia (who, before the club, had always struggled with school and sports and every activity known to man), being good at something felt really, really nice.

Malia and Jonah made their way back to the yard.

"What? How come you get ice cream?" yelled eight-year-old Fawn, the oldest Gregory child, upon seeing Jonah's chocolate-dipped cone. She angrily crossed her arms.

"YEAH!" echoed Plum and Piper, the six-year-old Gregory twins. "Not fair!"

"Don't worry, I brought enough for everyone," said Malia, holding the box aloft.

"Not so fast. Everyone has to sit down before they can have some," said Bree with authority. As one of five siblings, Bree was an expert at dealing with little kids and generally navigating chaos. Immediately, everyone sat, and Dot distributed the cones.

Malia also remembered a time — around the same point when boogers were enough to trigger a meltdown — when a gig like this would have driven her and her friends over the edge. But now they could watch four children and actually enjoy doing it.

As the small ones devoured their ice cream, Malia craned her neck to peer over the chain-link fence, trying to catch a glimpse of the neighbors. The house next door was small and blue, with a gray-shingled roof and some spindly ever-green trees dotting the backyard. To most anyone, it looked like a regular old house. But to Malia, it was a place of endless wonder.

It wasn't the home itself that was magical, but the people who lived there, particularly one Connor Kelly (aka the only boy worth loving). That house was the place where he woke up each morning and played video games and ate waffles. Con-nor's jeans—the very same jeans he casually stuck his hands in the pockets of—were somewhere inside, along with his backpack and his T-shirts and his bike and his toothbrush. The toothbrush that touched his beautiful smile. Malia shivered. It was almost too much to handle.

"Any sightings?" asked Dot.

"Not yet," said Malia. But there was still hope.

For years, Malia had watched Connor float through the halls of Playa del Mar's public school system the same way her older sister watched the shoe sales at the local mall—with a laser focus. But now, thanks to the Gregory gig, the unthinkable had happened: Malia could observe him in his natural habitat. That is, if he ever came outside.

"MOM!" yelled the Gregory twins, at the sound of a car in the driveway.

Mrs. Gregory appeared at the gate, where a peaceful, controlled scene awaited her. This was the magic of babysitting. By this point, Jonah's accident seemed like a distant memory. Any traces of sugar had been discarded. This was a skill they had learned over time—the ways of the artful cleanup. In the early days, the parents might return home to find their children spinning wildly, like sugar-addled tops. But today, all Mrs. Gregory saw were the smiling faces of her four beloved children and the three somewhat older children who had kept them alive and relatively happy for the last few hours.

"I'll definitely be calling you again soon," said Mrs. Gregory as she counted out a stack of crisp bills. "My sister invited me to a luncheon next weekend, and we'll need someone to watch the kids."

"Of course!" Malia said.

"We'd love to," Bree added, nodding so vigorously that her dangling iridescent gemstone earrings twinkled in the light.

As the girls started down the driveway, Malia saw something

from the corner of her eye. It was orange. It was moving. OH MY GOD IT WAS HIM.

The orange blob was none other than Connor Kelly, sauntering down his front lawn. The only thing standing between them was the Gregorys' chain-link fence (and about a stratosphere's worth of middle school politics, but really, who was counting?). Malia couldn't breathe. Her excitement level was like she'd seen a pop star and a movie star and a YouTube star and an actual star from the sky, all at the same time.

"Hi!" Malia said, so softly she barely heard it herself. It reminded her of how sometimes, when she ordered at the school cafeteria, some boy would place his order at the exact same moment as she did, but speak way louder, and no one would hear her voice.

"Hi?" Malia squeaked, a little louder.

Connor didn't seem to notice.

"Hi!" Malia said, at a volume that was unfortunately loud. This time Connor looked up.

"Oh, hey," he said, brushing his floppy hair off his forehead.

A bird chirped. Malia swore the sun began to shine a little brighter. Or was she just about to pass out? HOW WAS HE REAL?

"Um, okay," Malia said.

"Okay what?" Connor said.

"You know, just saying hi. Hi!"

"Hi," said Connor.

In her frequent daydreams of this situation, Malia was bursting with topics to discuss with imaginary Connor. But now, faced with real Connor, she couldn't think of a single thing to say. She glanced awkwardly down at her sneaker. Luckily, Connor interrupted the silence.

"So, I just found out I'm going to a concert," he said.

"Right now?" Malia asked. Maybe she could go, too.

"No, in three weeks," he said. "Veronica's coming to the Arts Center."

Malia gasped. Veronica (simply "Veronica," no last name necessary) was the biggest superstar imaginable. In the past year, she and her blue hair had skyrocketed to fame unlike anything ever witnessed before. Even Bree had virtually abandoned her love for Taylor Swift when faced with the glory of Veronica.

"Oh! Yeah, me too," said Malia. The lie escaped before she could realize what was happening.

Truth be told, Malia had never really caught Veronica fever. She thought Veronica was just *okay*, with her endless rotating wardrobe and her larger-than-life concerts. But Malia vowed then and there that no matter what it took, she would be at that show. It was the event of a lifetime—not because of Veronica, but because of Connor.

"Yeah, Charlotte's dad got a box for the concert, and everyone is going," said Connor. "Aidan, Bobby, Violet, Mo . . ."

"And me!" said Malia, with perhaps a bit too much force. "So I'll definitely see you there."

"Yeah. Sounds great," said Connor, sweeping his floppy hair away from his perfectly sun-kissed forehead.

"I can't wait! I mean, to see Veronica. I mean, of course." Malia started walking backward, away from the fence. "Enjoy the rest of your day!" As she tried to scurry away before any more words could escape her mouth, she stumbled over a tiny shrub. She quickly popped back up and retreated in a manner that she hoped looked very calm but feared looked rather rushed and awkward. Malia returned to the sidewalk where her friends were waiting and hoped she wasn't blushing too hard.

They walked in silence for another block, until they were sure it was safe.

"Oh my god," Malia stage-whispered. She thought she might hyperventilate.

"Are you okay?" Dot asked.

"You guys. There is a Veronica concert in two weeks, and Connor is going," Malia practically exploded.

Bree stopped in her tracks. "VERONICA?"

"Clearly, we have to go," Malia concluded.

"Veronica?" Bree repeated. "Is coming. Here?" She clutched her chest, like she had just been told something very profound.

"Yes, she's giving a huge concert at the Arts Center," Dot said matter-of-factly. "It was announced weeks ago."

"THE Veronica. In Playa del Mar." Bree was still trying to make sense of this.

"I think she's incredibly overhyped." Dot sighed. "I mean, I appreciate how she tries to stand for female empowerment, but her songs are very formulaic."

"But you listen to her," said Malia, shooting Dot a look. She knew for a fact that it was true.

"I like to stay up-to-date on popular culture," Dot argued. "I am not, technically, a fan."

"I CAN'T BELIEVE VERONICA IS COMING HERE!" Bree exclaimed.

"Yes, and everyone will be there," Malia added. "Including us."

"We have to go! How much are tickets? How do we buy them? Can we do this now?" Bree spoke, rapid-fire.

"The concert will probably have a decent concession stand," Dot conceded.

"And it will give me so much to talk about with Connor," Malia said wistfully. "Something to really connect over."

"How close do you think we can get? WHAT IF I COULD HUG HER OR EVEN JUST TOUCH HER HAND?" Bree continued to talk at a heightened volume.

"That's exactly how I feel about Connor," Malia said.

"Malia." Bree stopped in her tracks, and grabbed Malia by the shoulders. "We are talking about VERONICA. Like, an actual angel that is coming to our town to grace us with her presence. This is so much bigger than Connor."

"I'll never understand what you see in him," said Dot. "He seems very . . . one-dimensional."

"He doesn't even have any pets," Bree added.

Malia just sighed. Ordinarily, her friends were always on the same page, but when it came to matters of the heart, Malia was used to being on her own. Love was so far beyond reason. It was meant to be experienced, not understood.

First, though, she would have to experience this concert.

Malia didn't care what it took. She would babysit every day —heck, she would babysit every hour—until that concert rolled around. She was going to be there, and it was going to be amazing.

CHAPTER TWO

Bree

Bree Robinson could barely remember a time when she had felt this happy, although she supposed she felt pretty happy a lot of the time. Still, the most wonderful thing was about to happen—something even more wonderful than Veronica coming to Playa del Mar. Bree had been granted permission to adopt her very own cat.

Her mom had okayed it, on the condition that it couldn't interfere with Bree's ability to help out around the house. But how hard could a cat really be? You just had to feed it and love it and hug it and occasionally change its litter while holding your nose with one hand. A cat wasn't like a child, which actually required attention and sometimes even bribery. After babysitting, Bree figured, having a cat should be a breeze.

No longer would she have to feel insulted when Chocolate

Pudding, the family cat, ignored her displays of affection. Her *own* cat would never do such a thing. Her own cat would love her and snuggle with her and be her very best friend. Her own cat might even wear a hoodie. With sparkles! Bree couldn't wait.

All day long, she could barely concentrate on school. This was her biggest life dream come true. (Well, technically her biggest life dream was the one where she discovers Veronica is her long-lost sister, and Veronica lets Bree borrow all her shoes and clothes and joins forces to help open a cat ranch, where hundreds of cats could roam and play in total happiness, forever. But this slightly more realistic dream—adopting a cat *of her very own*—was pretty high up there.)

But now the moment was finally here. Bree was on her way to meet her future cat.

Bree, Malia, and Dot raced through the mall, with Bree leading the way, and Bree's mom trailing somewhere behind them.

"Are you sure it's a good idea to get a cat right now?" Malia asked. "I've booked us for four new gigs this week alone to help raise money for the concert."

"It's fine," Bree said. "I can totally handle it. The cat will probably nap all the time, anyway."

Nothing was going to rain on her cat parade. Not even Veronica.

They sped right by the other shops without so much as a glance until they reached the entrance to MeowTown, the neighborhood cat café.

"YES!" Bree yelled, so loudly it might have been heard in outer space. She inhaled. It smelled like kitty litter and endless possibilities. She breathed in so deeply that some airborne fur went up her nose, and she sneezed. She was in heaven.

MeowTown functioned just like an animal shelter. It took in homeless cats, provided vet care and shelter, and offered the added bonus of letting the public hang out with the cats until they found forever homes. All of the cats at MeowTown were up for adoption, and the staff was knowledgeable about every cat's story. Bree had been to MeowTown too many times to count, but she had never before gone with the mission of actually adopting one.

The girls scanned the café. There was an orange cat, a super-fat gray cat, a skinny black cat, a white cat with fluffy fur, and a trio of striped kittens. There was a cat with tortoiseshell fur, and even a Russian blue cat, which was called blue but was actually kind of gray. Bree stopped to say hello to each one.

"Do you have any idea what you're looking for?" asked Dot. "I mean, did you do any research?"

"Research? On what?" Bree asked, perplexed. "They're cats. I love them all."

"But don't they have, like, different temperaments or whatever?" Dot asked.

Was there any truth to this? Bree just shrugged. A cat was a cat. And a cat was wonderful.

Looking at face after feline face, Bree wondered how she would ever make a decision. How could she choose just one? It was like being asked to wear only purple or eat only gummy frogs for the rest of her life.

But then, she saw it.

All the way in the corner, a very creepy creature was huddled in the back of a hollow scratching tower. It didn't have any fur, and its skin was pink and wrinkly. It had huge yellow eyes and enormous ears that stood tall on top of its head, like a vampire bat.

Was it even a cat?

All around her, the other cats were busy romping, playing, and being petted by visitors. But the vampire cat-bat was all alone. At once, Bree's heart broke. She knew how it felt to be ignored, when all around you everyone else was doing cute or impressive things and you seemed invisible. She often felt overlooked in her giant family, and it was a sad sort of feeling.

She and the cat locked eyes. Bree loved it immediately.

"Hi, little friend!" said Bree, by way of greeting.

She approached the scratching tower.

"Ew," said Dot.

"I think there's something wrong with that one," said Malia.

"There is nothing wrong with her!" said Bree. She felt insulted on the maybe-cat's behalf.

Dot crouched down so she was close enough to read the tag around the cat's neck. "McDuffin. What kind of name is that?"

"It sounds like fast food," said Malia.

"You know I love fast food, but that sounds like a mistake," said Dot.

"I'm in love with her!" said Bree, clasping her hands together.

"You're in love . . . with that?" asked Malia, wrinkling her face up like she smelled a fart. "Are you sure?"

"We're not even sure what that is," said Dot. "Is it a cat?"

"It is the most beautiful cat," said Bree. The cat visibly

brightened. Watching this cat, Bree suddenly understood how Malia felt about Connor Kelly. It was like seeing a unicorn in a forest, and then having all your friends insist it was just a regular horse. Why couldn't they see the magic?

Bree's mom, who had lingered silently a few feet away from the girls, finally spoke up. "Oh," she said. "That's, um, that's interesting."

Bree sighed. "Everything about her is perfect."

"I beg to disagree," said Dot. She began counting off the reasons on her fingers. "For one, it doesn't have any fur. Two, do we need to be concerned that it's standing like that? Like it wants to maybe kill us? Three, its expression is . . . highly concerning."

"No! Her face is sweet," argued Bree. "So sweet and wrinkly. She just needs lots of hugs."

"And a sweater," said Malia.

"Oh my goodness, yes! Or a hoodie!" Bree was already planning her extensive wardrobe, mentally putting aside some of her former dolls' clothes that might be a good fit. Bree had dreamed about dressing up her cat, but this hairless cat would actually require it!

"Excuse me, um, Bartholomeow?" Bree called to the nearest volunteer. "Can you tell me more about this one?"

The volunteer shuffled over to the scratching tower. He looked to be a college student, and his name tag read *BARTHOLOMEW*. (Though Bree had clearly misread it as "Bartholo-meow," which only added to her excitement.)

"This here is a sphynx cat," he said, "a very special breed."

"You can say that again," said Dot, prompting a giggle from Malia.

"Sphynx cats are highly social cats that enjoy more attention than your typical housecat," Bartholomew explained. "They tend to get along well with other animals, and they have LOTS of energy. They love to be held and snuggled, almost like dogs!"

Attention? Snuggling? Bree was sold.

"I'll take her!" said Bree, with the kind of enthusiasm usually reserved for people on game shows or reality shows or home makeover shows or really any kind of show where people win stuff.

"Um, perhaps he can tell us some more facts about this specific cat before we sign on the dotted line," Bree's mom cut in.

"Yes, it's best to be absolutely sure of your decision." Bartholomew nodded somberly. "We're looking to find each of these animals forever homes, and we wouldn't want to cause the cat any undue stress."

"Where did this particular animal come from?" Bree's mom asked.

"McDuffin was an owner surrender." Bartholomew frowned. "McDuffin is quite young, you see, but the original owner had change-in-life circumstances and could no longer handle pet ownership."

This prompted an "Aww" from Bree.

Bartholomew paused before adding, "And neither could either of the families who adopted him since."

"I'm sorry, did you say this cat has been returned *three* times?" Dot asked.

Malia and Dot elbowed each other.

"Now, not exactly. I mean, technically yes, but not for any real reason!" Bartholomew added quickly. "No, no, there's nothing wrong with McDuffin. McDuffin just has the worst luck."

"And the worst name," Malia added.

"And the craziest eyes," Dot continued.

"And the sweetest face!" Bree concluded. "I LOVE YOU, HONEY MUFFIN!" she whispered at the cat's face.

The cat hissed softly.

"Anyway, it's best to make sure you and the cat have good feelings about each other," Bartholomew insisted.

Bree turned her attention back to Bartholomew, and then to her mom. "Yes, I'm absolutely sure. This is the cat for me."

Bree's mom hesitated, then nodded.

"All right, let's make it official!" Bartholomew clapped his hands and led Bree's mom over to the front counter so she could fill out the adoption paperwork.

While her mom took care of the boring stuff, Bree picked out a rhinestone collar and a trio of sparkly toy mice. She got a little choked up, imagining her new best friend romping joyfully around her room with the new toys. Bree couldn't wait for McDuffin to discover her wonderful new life. Just a few moments later, McDuffin was in a cat carrier, bound for the Robinson house.

"So you have a new baby," Malia said, eyeing the feline cargo. "How does it feel?"

"I can't believe it!" Bree said. "This is the best day of my life."

"What are you going to name her?" asked Dot. "I mean, clearly you can't keep calling her McDuffin."

"I shall name her . . ." Bree paused for effect. "Veronica."

"I'm sensing a theme here," said Dot.

It was only fitting. For years, Bree had tried to change the family cat Chocolate Pudding's name to Taylor Swift and had been met with much resistance. But now she could name her own cat whatever she wanted. From this moment forward, Veronica would forever be known as Veronica.

"I suppose this Veronica doesn't have a last name, either?" Malia asked.

"MEOW," Veronica said, somewhat aggressively.

"Okay, then," said Malia. "No last name necessary."

"You guys, thank you so much for being part of my big day!" Bree said, getting a little choked up. "You're going to be the best cat aunts ever."

"We wouldn't have missed it for the world." Dot smiled. "Although I'm not sure I'm cut out to be a cat aunt. But I'll certainly try my best."

"We should celebrate," said Malia.

"Ooh, yes! Do you guys want to hit up the food court?" Dot asked.

"Yeah!" Malia visibly brightened at the mention of food.

"We should probably get going," Bree said, tilting her head toward Veronica, who was now rubbing her bald, wrinkly head against the inside of the carrier door. "You know, introduce her to her new home and all."

"Oh, right," Malia said.

"Yeah. But you guys go on without me!" Bree said.

She gave each of her friends a one-armed hug with her right arm, with the cat case cradled in her left. There was something bittersweet about this moment. Of course she was sad to miss out on the food court, but she was embarking on a much bigger journey — the path of pet parenthood.

The entire car ride home, Bree whispered into the cat carrier, sharing her hopes and dreams. She told Veronica about all the beautiful toys waiting back at home, and how they would wear matching outfits and sleep in Bree's big, fluffy bed. She told her about all the songs she would sing and the musical numbers Veronica could participate in. There was even talk of a sequined hoodie the perfect size for a cat.

At last, they arrived home. Bree could hardly believe this was it: the beautiful moment when they started their new life, together.

"And this," Bree said, opening the door to her bedroom, "is your new home. What do you think?"

The cat did not answer.

Bree placed the cat carrier in the center of her room and opened the tiny door.

"Welcome home, Veronica!"

The cat made no move to exit. She just sat there, scowling.

"Veronica! This is where you live now."

More scowling.

Bree sat on her bed, waiting for the cat to emerge. But she showed no sign of movement. Bree tried to think of what she would do if a new babysitting charge was being shy. Maybe a game of show-and-tell would liven things up. She started wandering around the room, holding up objects.

She grabbed a stuffed giraffe off of a shelf. "This is Wallace," she said. "I met him at a carnival when I was seven. He's kind of a secret. I've slept next to him every night since I was in kindergarten and I'm not about to stop now. But now that you live here, if you want to cuddle with me instead, well, we can talk about that."

Veronica blinked.

Bree grabbed a book from her desk. "This is my chemistry textbook. I'm not sure what it's doing out on my desk right now, because I hate it." She slipped it into her backpack, where she could no longer see it. "That's better."

Next, Bree wandered back over to the bed. "This is my favorite pillow." She held up a pillow that her seventeen-year-old stepsister, Ariana, had given her for her last birthday. It was navy blue, with lots of very shiny silver sequins sewed all over it, like tiny little mirrors. "Isn't it pretty?" The pillow sparkled in the light.

"MEOW-MEOW!" Veronica came bounding out of the case. "MEEEEEEEEEROW!" The cat headed straight toward her, a look of pure fury in her giant yellow eyes. Bree had never seen anything move so fast in her life. She was so shocked, she dropped the pillow.

"MEEEEEEEEEW!" Veronica landed on top of the pillow, where she began attacking it with her very sharp claws. Mirrored sequins flew into the air, along with clouds of stuffing. It was the most destructive thing Bree had ever seen. She stood there, stunned.

Bree had loved that pillow for as long as she'd had it, and she'd loved cats for, well, her entire life. She had pictured a very different homecoming. Instead, she stood helplessly, watching as her perfect day was destroyed in seconds.

She had expected to spend this day petting Veronica, dressing her in various dolls' clothes while softly singing her songs from *Cats the Musical*. Veronica, clearly, had a different idea.

CHAPTER THREE

Dot

Dot stared into her beaker with the same intensity her mother (a practicing clairvoyant) used to gaze into her crystal ball. Most likely, it was growing up in a home surrounded by crystals and candles and charts about meridians and chakras that had pushed Dot toward her love of hard data and irrefutable facts. While she excelled in all subjects, from literature to algebra to Latin, science was her thing. Dot preferred the school's science lab to all other places. To her, there was nothing more satisfying than being surrounded by test tubes and chemicals and scales, conducting experiments that would ultimately lead to only one right answer.

Today, her chemistry class was working on a very simple assignment, the distillation of wood. Dot already knew the outcome: after the wood was heated, it would decompose, forming charcoal and vapors. Still, she completed every step, charting her progress along the way.

Dot was glad that today's assignment was such a simple one because she was tired. She had spent the previous night babysitting for the Gomez family, new clients they had taken on to help drum up money for Veronica concert tickets. Dot didn't like to take jobs on school nights, especially two nights in a row like she had this week, but she supposed it was worth it until the concert.

To be very clear, Dot did not care about Veronica. She hardly ever listened to her music, except sometimes ironically. Okay, fine, Dot could admit that some of the songs were catchy, and even that they had the ability to put her in a sort of infectiously good mood. There was a time and place for Veronica music, like when attempting to exercise or perform a mindless task. But Dot was most excited about the concert itself, because the venue had excellent junk food—popcorn, funnel cakes, and the best chicken fingers you could imagine. Her mom hadn't made any progress on her rules against allowing gluten or animal products or processed sugar into the house, so Dot needed to seize every opportunity she had.

"Looking good," said Mr. Frang, nodding as he passed Dot's lab table. The head of the science department, Mr. Frang was a tall man with a gray beard that reminded Dot of an elf. It was obvious that Dot was his favorite student, though she knew he tried to act impartial.

Dot squinted her eyes, concentrating with laser focus, but her mind wasn't on today's experiment. In truth, it was somewhere else entirely: thinking about the upcoming science fair.

The middle school science fair was a very big deal, as it was the gateway to everything important in the science community. The winner of the school fair would go on to compete at the regional level, followed by the state level and, eventually, against the entire nation. Students who competed at the national level were scouted for special programs and awards, and were often the ones who were awarded scholarships when the time came to apply for college.

Dot knew she was only in middle school, but still, she liked to plan ahead. Despite her mom's psychic abilities, it would be hard for her to afford college tuition, and Dot was determined to work it out on her own. This was just one of many factors that made it particularly troubling that she hadn't yet come up with a winning idea.

Luckily, the other students at Playa del Mar weren't particularly competitive. She could already predict what everyone else would do. All the usual suspects would be covered: a homemade radio, a chart of the various types of fingerprints, an exploration of how a blindfold changes the relationship to taste and smell. That was all fine and good. But she needed to innovate. She needed something that would trump them all.

This was game time. Crunch time. Go time. All of the times. This was it.

Just as Dot was getting lost in a daydream in which she won the national science fair and was receiving a medal of honor at the White House, the door to the science lab creaked open.

Principal Davies set one foot inside the room.

"Everyone, I'd like you to meet a new student here at Playa del Mar." She stepped aside to allow said student to enter. "This is Pigeon de Palma."

Dot looked up to see a very pretty girl. She had super-long, wavy brown hair, almost like a darker version of Dot's hair. She wore a black T-shirt emblazoned with a faded golden lightning bolt, black skinny jeans, and the coolest ankle boots Dot had ever seen. They were black leather, with teeny tiny gold studs snaking all around them, in complicated designs. Around the ankles, they had three thin straps, each ending with a delicate gold buckle. Dot had seen shoes like that in magazines but never in person.

"Hi, everyone," Pigeon said, offering the classroom a little wave. Her voice was sort of low and gravely, but very cute. "I'm so excited to be here."

"Welcome, Pigeon!" said Mr. Frang.

Dot wasn't sure what to make of this Pigeon person. It was very rare for Playa del Mar to welcome new students after the start of the school year. It was even weirder for them to look . . . cool.

"Pigeon just moved here from New York City," added Principal Davies, which was pretty much the only thing she could have said to push Dot over the edge. It was Dot's dream to live in NYC someday—heck, at this point it was her dream even just to visit—and Pigeon had spent her formative years there? This was so unfair. No wonder she seemed so sophisticated. No wonder her boots were so cool. "I'm sure you'll all do your best to make her feel welcome," the principal concluded, leaving Pigeon to fend for herself.

Pigeon circled the lab tables, looking for a place to sit. Dot turned her attention back to the distillation of wood. There would be plenty of time to analyze the new girl, but for now, there was work to do.

"Do you mind if I join you?" said a gravelly voice.

Dot looked up. Pigeon was speaking to her.

"Um, I don't really do group assignments," Dot said. She

wasn't trying to be rude; it was true. Unless the experiment absolutely called for lab partners, Dot always preferred to work alone.

"It's all right, we already did this experiment at my old school," Pigeon said, casually tossing her long, wavy hair. A spicy fragrance wafted through the air. Dot immediately recognized it as a designer perfume her own hippie mother wouldn't let her buy.

"Well, the experiment is basically completed, so there'd be nothing left for you to do anyway," Dot said.

"I can just observe," Pigeon said as she pulled up a chair.

Dot inhaled, trying not to let her newfound audience faze her.

"At my old school, distillation of wood was actually a *sixth*-grade experiment," Pigeon said. Her condescending tone was not lost on Dot. "I wonder if I'll be repeating a lot of the old curriculum here. Especially because science has always been kind of my thing."

"Science has always been *my* thing," said Dot. "Which is why, outside of the school's curriculum, I've been conducting research on my own for years now."

Pigeon impatiently tapped her fingernails on the lab table,

breaking Dot's concentration. Dot noticed they were painted a sort of green metallic oil-slick color that Dot had never seen before. Even Pigeon's nail polish was fancy.

"So, where in New York did you live?" Dot asked.

"We lived on the Upper West Side," Pigeon said, "but my school was on the Upper East."

"Wow. That must have been amazing," said Dot, while her head kept singing *unfair, unfair, unfair.*

"This town seems . . ." Pigeon trailed off, as though searching for the right word. "Cute."

The way she said the word "cute" made it clear it wasn't a compliment.

Dot wanted to leave this town more than anyone, but she didn't appreciate this stranger rolling up and trash-talking it on her very first day. Who did this person think she was?

Dot's hands flew across the equipment, attempting to complete the assignment as quickly as possible so she could be free of this situation.

"I'm going to start handing back the quizzes from yesterday," said Mr. Frang. "Please don't let them distract you from your experiments. If you have any questions, of course I'm available after class."

Dot didn't even bother to look when the paper landed on her table. She never got anything less than an A, especially in science.

"Hm. B-plus," said Pigeon, staring at the quiz.

"What?" Dot snapped to attention. "There must be some kind of mistake." Dot did not get Bs, ever. She hardly ever got A-minuses. Bs were for the hoi polloi. The fact that Dot even knew what "hoi polloi" meant only further cemented her status as an A student.

But sure enough, there it was: her quiz, with a big red B-plus on top of it.

How had this happened? She knew she'd been kind of exhausted this week, with babysitting eating into her homework time, but still. This was unprecedented.

Once again, Principal Davies appeared at the door.

"Pigeon, I'm sorry. As it turns out, I need you to come with me. I forgot I have another part of the orientation packet to go through together."

"You know, I actually interned for Elon Musk last summer," said Pigeon as she stood and pushed her chair in. "You know, the guy who started SpaceX? And Tesla? And who is, like, an investor and businessperson—"

"I know who Elon Musk is," Dot interrupted, annoyed.

"If you ever need somebody to tutor you, I'm sure we could work something out."

Dot was flabbergasted. Pigeon smiled. "It's been awfully nice chatting with you. I'm sure I'll see you around." And with that, she turned and walked away.

"Yeah, likewise," murmured Dot.

Dot kept her eyes on her beaker, fighting the urge to watch Pigeon as she walked away.

Dot knew one thing for sure: She did not like this Pigeon person. It wasn't just her ridiculous first name, although that probably didn't help. It was—Dot couldn't believe what she was thinking, was she turning into her mother?—her aura.

Pigeon had very bad energy.

You're being ridiculous, Dot thought. *You don't even know her. It's her first day at a new school and she's just trying to be impressive to make friends.*

Still, this felt like that moment in a movie, where the main character meets her nemesis. Dot wanted to remain open and kind. She wanted to know her story. But she was, Dot hated to admit, experiencing a feeling she had never felt before. She was intrigued. She was jealous. She was conflicted. For perhaps the first time ever, she was seriously intimidated.

CHAPTER FOUR

MALIA

Malia watched as Connor Kelly sauntered across the cafeteria, blue plastic lunch tray in hand. He gave her a slight nod and then sat down with the other boys on the soccer team. Malia sighed. He was so close and yet so far away.

Malia remembered a time, not too long ago, when she and Connor barely exchanged words. Back then, she sometimes wondered if he even knew her name. Now he said at least three sentences to her each week. That, Malia thought, was progress.

Still, so much about Connor remained a mystery. He was like some exotic endangered species Malia could only observe from a safe distance. Across rooms . . . on social media . . . but rarely up close and personal. But now she had places to run into Connor—like the cafeteria, or the Gregory house, or, if everything went according to plan, the Veronica concert.

She had spent all of her waking moments (and also some of her sleeping ones) dreaming for the past three days about the concert and how it might go. The darkness, the neon lights, the fog, the music, the dancing. Malia shivered. The thought of dancing in Connor Kelly's proximity was almost too much to handle.

But of course, before that could happen, she had to buy the tickets. Malia had lined up jobs like crazy, posting on social media to drum up some new clients. Plus, Bree's mom agreed to let her babysit her brother, Bailey, three days a week, and Mrs. Gregory had booked Malia for three upcoming jobs, which meant money and a potential Connor sighting in one.

Shoko and Mo arrived at the table, placing their trays down with a clatter. Shoko and Mo were pretty much inseparable, and they always sat at the same lunch table as Malia and Bree. Malia snapped out of her daydream.

"What are you wearing to the concert?" asked Mo urgently. The entire school had caught Veronica fever. The concert was all anybody could talk about.

"I don't know," said Malia, though she had, of course, been obsessing about this very topic for days. Maybe if they had any money left over from buying the ticket, she could get a new outfit. "What are you guys wearing?"

"Ugh, who knows? It's such an event. We're going shopping this weekend!" said Shoko, waving her hands around as if she found this stressful. Her parents gave her a seemingly unlimited allowance to spend on things like concert wear. Malia wondered, as she often had, what that must be like.

"Hiiiii," said Bree, suddenly appearing with her lunch. She put her tray down and pulled up a seat next to Malia.

Bree removed her studded jean jacket and hung it on the back of her chair. Malia noticed that she had tiny little scratches all over her arms.

"Oh my god, what happened to you?" said Malia, with genuine concern.

"Oh, just Veronica." Bree sighed. "There was an incident this morning, involving glitter eyeliner and a very violent feline outburst. That cat's claws are no joke."

"Wow. I'm . . . sorry to hear that," Malia said.

"It's okay," said Bree with a shrug. "I mean, it's actually not okay. But I'm fine."

Dot approached the lunch table and put her tray down next to Malia's.

"Can I sit with you guys?" she asked.

This was an irregular occurrence. For as long as Malia could remember, Dot had always sat at a different lunch table, with the honors students who thought they were a little bit smarter than everyone else. Malia had learned not to take it personally, as lunchtime politics were complicated.

"What? You're deigning to sit with the non-honors students?" Malia teased. "At LUNCH? What is going on here?"

Dot rolled her eyes. "This annoying new girl is sitting at my table, and I just . . . can't."

"Well, I'm glad you're here," Malia said, "Because we were just talking about gearing up for the Veronica concert and I have booked all the jobs in the land."

Dot took a deep breath.

"Okay. To be clear, I still need time to focus on homework right now. Not to mention the science fair." She paused before adding, "And for the last time, I do not like Veronica."

"To each her own," said Malia. "But I, for one, will babysit every second I can until we are all sitting front row at that concert."

And she meant every word.

Malia arrived home floating on a cloud. She had taken to listening to Veronica on her way to and from anywhere, as she found it inspired her to make her dreams a reality.

"I saw your face on my phone. You just won't leave me alone," sang

Veronica. Of course, this made Malia think of Connor. *"Social me-me-me-me-media. But everything's about you."*

Malia felt so joyful that she almost didn't mind when she bumped into her sister, Chelsea, the seventeen-year-old human equivalent of an evil snake, making her way through the front hallway.

"Why, if it isn't the smaller version of me!" said Chelsea. This was her idea of the ultimate compliment. It was also a stark contrast from the usual insults Chelsea flung Malia's way.

Immediately, Malia was suspicious.

"What do you want?" she asked.

"The real question is: What do YOU want? What do you want, little sister, from your life?"

Yes, Chelsea was up to something. But really, Chelsea was *always* up to something. Previously, she had formed a rival baby-sitting business and attempted to put Malia and her friends out of business. Who knew what sort of terrible scheme she was devising now.

"Right now, all I want is to go to my room," Malia said, then added, "Where you aren't allowed."

Malia's eyes landed on the large framed family portrait that hung near the front door. The entire family — Mom, Dad, Chelsea, and Malia stood dressed in white and beaming for the camera. It looked so happy, and so misleading. Malia could barely remember another time when she had been in Chelsea's presence and made that same expression.

"Oh, Malia. When I was your age, I was so ambitious. I was already mapping out my future. I think it's about time you started to do the same."

Malia tried to go around her, but Chelsea blocked her path.

"MOM!" Malia yelled, which was the easiest way she could think of to make this situation stop.

"Yes?" called their mother. Moments later she appeared, with a celery stalk in her hand.

"Chelsea is harassing me about my future again," said Malia.

"That is an unfair assessment. I was just trying to offer Malia a chance to follow in my unusually accomplished footsteps."

"I can make my own footsteps!" Malia protested.

"By joining our team at Abernathy Inc." Chelsea paused, waiting for a reaction.

"Wait, what?" asked Malia. This was news to her.

"Ramona and I are looking for a new junior intern," Chelsea continued, "and I think Malia would be a perfect fit."

Chelsea had recently accepted an internship with Ramona

Abernathy, a retired tech mogul and the wealthiest woman in all of Playa del Mar. Even though she was technically retired, Ramona was still a very busy woman. As Chelsea explained it, she worked as a consultant on all sorts of projects and sat on the board of many organizations. Malia didn't quite understand what that meant, but she gathered that it was important. And working for Ramona was impressive, by any measure.

"Oh my goodness! What an honor," said their mom.

Still, Malia was skeptical. This was Chelsea, after all. Her big sister was known for achievement in every area except kindness. Doing Malia favors was not a bullet point on her very long résumé. In fact, she wasn't even particularly inclined to include Malia in social activities, routinely excluding her from social gatherings *in their own house* and "forgetting" to wait for Malia to join the carpool home from school.

But now Chelsea was being nice? For no apparent reason? Something was amiss.

"I think this sounds like a wonderful opportunity!" said their mom, clapping her hands together as though she was at a Broadway show.

"Does it pay?" Malia asked.

"It pays to put it on your résumé," Chelsea said, rolling her eyes.

"That kind of experience is priceless," said their mother. Malia's mom worked as a career counselor, and this kind of thing was right up her alley.

"The internship is every Tuesday, Wednesday, and Thursday after school, plus Saturdays," said Chelsea.

"Whoa. Four days? But what about babysitting?" Malia asked. "And schoolwork? I'm already super busy." *And the Veronica concert is happening in a few weeks,* she silently added.

Chelsea snorted. "Like you've ever been serious about school. And look at me. I'm able to balance my internship with school, plus way more activities than you've ever done."

"Malia, I'm glad you're thinking about time management," said their mom.

"Yes, and I have a lot on my plate," said Malia. This was a phrase her mom used a lot, so Malia hoped it might work to her advantage.

"But time management is a great skill for you to work on," her mom concluded. "And this can be practice. Having an internship will teach you how to prioritize!"

"Unless you're afraid you can't do it," Chelsea added.

Malia sensed this was a fight she would never win. Plus, she hated when Chelsea acted superior. If Chelsea could balance everything, then surely Malia could, too.

"Okay, so how does it work? Do I have to apply?" she asked.

"Just come with me to the office on Thursday," Chelsea said. "I've already talked you up. You're my sister, and Ramona will love you."

"Could I, like, try it out first?" Malia asked. She was terrified of committing to something that would eat up four days of her week, without the promise of money or Connor or her friends or anything of the other things that brought joy.

"Malia, this is an opportunity hundreds of girls would kill for," Chelsea said. "It's a yes or a no."

Malia had never liked that phrase, about the things other girls would kill for. Anything involving killing was sure to be bad, including the sound of this internship. Still, she felt trapped. If she said no, she would look like a wimp in front of Chelsea. If she said yes, she just cut her available babysitting time in half, not to mention her funds. She had a concert to go to and Connor's heart to win.

"I don't know . . ." Malia waffled.

"The answer is yes," said her mom.

"Yes?" said Malia tentatively.

Her mom beamed. Chelsea smirked. Malia sighed.

Since she clearly had no choice in this matter, she figured

she might as well roll with it. With the art of babysitting firmly under her control, maybe it was time to expand her business sense by taking on a real-person job. Who knows what she'd learn, or what she'd be inspired to do? Maybe Ramona had the secrets to unlimited earning potential. She was about to find out.

CHAPTER FIVE

Bree

But the bonnet is so cute!" yelled Bree. "I don't understand what your problem is!" She held a glittery blue bonnet in the air, prompting the cat to dig his claws ever deeper into Bree's second-favorite sparkly pillow.

In the three short days Bree had owned him (the vet had informed them that Veronica was, in fact, a boy cat), Veronica had all but destroyed Bree's lifelong dream of feline parenthood. He had also, quite literally, destroyed her comforter, her fluffy white rug, her curtains, and everything that once sat on top of her desk.

Despite what Bartholomew had said, this particular sphynx cat had no interest in being hugged. He wasn't even a little bit cuddly. He didn't want to socialize with Chocolate Pudding, or with Bree, or really with anyone. He did, however, have a lot of energy.

"I love you!" Bree yelled, close to tears. "Why won't you let me love you?"

The cat stared at her menacingly, his giant yellow eyes glowing with what anyone who wasn't Bree would likely identify as pure evil.

Bree pounced on top of him, causing the cat to scratch at her arm. "You're supposed to want to be held!" she said. "Hugs are good for you!" Somehow, she managed to hold him for just long enough to squeeze the bonnet onto his head and secure it with the little elastic. Veronica made a sound not unlike a baby screaming.

Just then, there was a knock at her bedroom door.

"Bree, lovey?" her mom called from outside the locked door.

"Yes?" Bree called, trying to sound casual.

"I'm picking up Emma and Olivia from dance lessons, so it's time for you to hang out with Bailey until we get back. He needs help with his school project."

"Okay!" Bree called as Veronica ran in manic circles around her.

Bree's job was to babysit Bailey, especially now that the concert was approaching and she needed the extra money. But so far, it felt virtually impossible. How was Bree ever supposed to see human Veronica if she couldn't get cat Veronica under control?

"And it's taco night, so can you also take the stuff out of the fridge? I'll heat everything up as soon as I'm back."

"Uh-huh!" Bree said, her voice colored with fake sunshine.

"Okay! Everything is good with the cat?" Her mom sounded suspicious. How did she always know everything?

"Yep! Everything is great," Bree said as Veronica went into full-on attack mode with one of Bree's remaining pillows, sending stuffing flying through the air.

"Okay, then! I'm heading out. Come downstairs, okay?"

"Coming!" Bree said in a singsong voice, as she scrambled to pick up the bits of discarded stuffing and bury them securely in a trash bag.

Veronica meowed, pleased with himself.

Bree sighed.

"Look, I get that you had a rough kittenhood or whatever, but I love you now. You're safe here. You don't have to keep acting out. You have food and litter and toys and an entire wardrobe with outfits for every occasion and even accessories."

The cat meowed defiantly.

"I need you to, like, calm down."

Veronica blinked one time.

"Can you stay in here and not destroy everything? I have to go downstairs for a little bit to spend time with Bailey. I'm not abandoning you. I'll come back upstairs soon, okay?"

The cat sauntered in front of the door, daring her to open it.

"No, I need you to stay in here."

Bree felt very exasperated. She wondered what Taylor Swift would do in this situation. She carried her cats around in the airport and stuff, and they seemed so nice.

Bree had no choice but to resort to bribery. She opened a package of fish-flavored cat treats and threw one across the room. Veronica bounded after it, his bonnet sparkling all the way. Bree slipped out the door, closing it behind her.

Downstairs, she opened the fridge to find the ingredients she needed for taco night. Tortillas and all sorts of toppings—including her favorite: fish covered with her mom's signature marinade—sat in foil-covered dishes. Bree took each dish out of the fridge and lined them up on the counter. Bree loved taco night. She felt thankful that it would be a happy ending to what was turning out to be a very stressful day.

Once everything was set up, Bree headed to the family room, where Bailey sat on the couch, watching cartoons, eating popcorn, and having no idea how good his life was. He didn't have a psycho cat. He didn't have to hold down a job or even help out around the house. He just got to be nine years old, which seemed like a pretty good deal.

"What are you watching?" Bree asked.

"*Danger Duck Detective Agency*," Bailey said, never taking his eyes from the screen.

"Should you really be watching this right now? Mom said you needed help with your project."

"Yeah, but I'm almost done," Bailey countered. "It's a papier-mâché model of the Eiffel Tower. Mom already helped me make the base level and I just have to put another layer of paper on top."

"Okay, well, then maybe we should finish it together now, quickly, so we don't have to worry about it," Bree suggested. "You'll feel good once it's done." She purposefully left out the part where she wanted to get it over with as fast as possible so she could run back to check on her . . . challenging cat.

"Okay. It's in Marc's study," Bailey said with a shrug.

They headed into Bree's stepdad's office, where the lopsided, half-finished Eiffel Tower was on top of the desk, surrounded by decidedly less artistic things, like stacks of Marc's legal papers. Bree spread out the supplies, and they got to work. They were just getting into a good rhythm of layering on the paper strips, when Bailey suddenly looked surprised.

"What's that noise?" Bailey asked.

"I don't hear anything," Bree said.

"It sounds like a goose. Being strangled."

At that moment, something truly horrible-smelling made its way into Bree's nostrils.

"What is *that*?" said Bree, gagging. It was the worst thing Bree had ever smelled. It was even worse than diapers.

"Ewww! That is sick!" Bailey added, covering his nose and mouth with his hands.

They followed the smell out of the study, through the foyer and into the formal living room—the fanciest room in the house, where Bree and her siblings were usually not allowed to go. The scent grew stronger and stronger.

And then, she saw it.

Veronica—sparkly bonnet still on his head—was inside the grand piano. There he stood, perched on the strings of the enormous instrument, where he proceeded to puke directly into it.

"GAK! GAK! GAK!"

"Whoa," said Bailey. "Mom is going to kill you."

"VERONICAAAAA!" screamed Bree, sprinting to the piano and trying to grab the cat. But Veronica was too fast. He leaped out of the way and scurried out of the room, flying through the house until he was nowhere to be found.

Bree exited the living room in a stupor, following Veronica's path of destruction. In the short amount of time she had been with Bailey, Veronica had attacked a dining room chair and consumed all of the ingredients that were laid out for the family's fish taco night. Now the thrown-up fish tacos were marinating inside the piano.

"How did he even get out of my room?" Bree wondered aloud.

"Meow!" Bree turned around, hoping to see Veronica. Instead, she saw Chocolate Pudding, the family's furry orange cat. Chocolate Pudding used to annoy her, the way she was always licking her hind legs and minding her own business. Now Chocolate Pudding seemed so sane. Why, oh, why hadn't Bree realized how good things were before?

Bree missed her old life from three days ago. She missed doing crafts and seeing her friends and eating snacks and listening to the soundtrack from *Cats the Musical* on endless repeat in the comfort of her own bedroom. That is, her old bedroom—before a disturbed cat had taken over and turned it from a sanctuary to a stress factory. Bree loved animals; she even loved *this* animal. But that didn't change the fact that this whole cat adoption was the hardest thing she had ever done.

After doing her best to clean out the piano (which took more paper towels and more self-control than Bree had wielded before), she searched the house from top to bottom. Veronica was nowhere to be found. With a resigned sigh, she reasoned she might as well return to her other responsibility and go check on Bailey.

She entered Marc's office to see the tower had grown impressively in size.

"That looks great!" she exclaimed. At least something was going right.

Unfortunately, as she took a closer look, Bree saw the tower had something very, very wrong with it. There were a bunch of handwritten notes and little typed words all over it. *Damages . . . compensation . . . loss . . .*

Bree gasped as she fully accepted the sinking realization: The topmost layer of the papier-mâché tower was constructed from Marc's legal papers.

"Bailey! What kind of paper did you use for that?"

"I just took some of the pages from one of those big piles," he said, motioning to one of Marc's shelves.

"But that looks like one of Marc's briefs! It has lawyer words all over it."

"Don't worry, I'm going to paint over it," Bailey said. "No one will see them."

"That's not the point. The point is what if he needed that? Marc is going to be super mad!"

"Oh. Do you think that paper was, like, important?" Bailey asked.

Bree covered her face with her hands.

"Can't he just print a new one?"

"No, it had his notes all over it!"

"Oops?" said Bailey.

Bailey seemed remarkably unfazed by this exchange. Of course, Bree thought, because he could just go back to eating popcorn and being nine and not having to take responsibility for stuff. This was all Bree's fault, because she was supposed to be watching him. This entire day was a disaster. Before Veronica, babysitting had been the one thing she had under control. Now she suddenly felt like she was failing at everything.

Never one to hide from her problems, Bree sat in the front hallway, waiting for her mom to get home. As soon as she got back, Bree would tell her what happened. Her mom was going to be super mad. But Bree also needed her to tell her what to do.

"Why, hello there, Mom!" Bree said the moment the key turned in the lock.

Emma and Olivia ran past her, flaunting the joyful freedom of being children.

"What's wrong?" asked her mom, making a suspicious face.

"Who says that anything's wrong?"

"You. You're acting very odd right now. Why are you sitting on the floor like that? What happened?"

Bree started to cry. "Veronica-ate-the-tacos-and-puked-in-the-piano-and-Bailey-used-Marc's-brief-to-make-the-Eiffel-Tower-and-I'm-sorry!"

"Bree." Her mom looked tired. "Remember what we talked about. Bree, I know you love Veronica, but I need you to get this cat under control! Our agreement was that the cat couldn't interfere with your ability to help out around the house. Your job is to watch Bailey at least three days a week, and you promised this wouldn't interfere. This is exactly the kind of situation . . ."

Bree wailed with grief.

"It's okay, it's okay," her mom said. "I mean, it's not okay, but no one is hurt and that's what's important."

"I'm sorry," Bree said. "Please don't make me give up the cat."

She thought of the terrible things he was probably doing to her bedroom at that very moment.

"All right, but consider this a warning," her mom told her. "We need to get this under control, otherwise the cat can't stay."

Bree hoped that she and Veronica could come to an understanding. She wasn't sure exactly how, but for now, she was willing to be hopeful.

CHAPTER SIX

MALIA

"WHERE is the THING?" yelled Ramona, her voice echoing from the other room.

"What thing?" hissed Malia under her breath.

"Thing finding is totally your job," Chelsea said with an unhelpful shrug.

"How am I supposed to know what the thing is? I've been working here for, like, an hour."

"I was once in your place, and I survived. I believe in you. You'll figure it out." And with that, Chelsea went back to typing whatever document she was working on.

"I'M WAAAAAAAITING!" trilled Ramona.

It hadn't even been an hour, and already Malia deeply regretted giving in to the pressure to join Abernathy Inc. Ramona was bossy, demanding, and confusing. Predictably, Chelsea was no help. Who was her mother kidding with this? Malia was a middle-schooler. She was meant to be outside, hanging with her friends, or inside, babysitting minors and earning money for things like concerts, or else roaming the mall in search of nothing in particular. She wasn't meant to be in this office, searching for utterly unidentified objects.

But for now, she needed to find the thing. Malia scooted very quickly into the adjacent room, Ramona's private office. Ramona was a grandmother's age, but she wasn't like any grandma Malia had ever seen. For starters, she had the energy of a twenty-two-year-old.

"Hi, Ramona, what can I help you find?" asked Malia.

"The THING!" yelled Ramona. "I simply cannot find it." She banged her hands on her enormous lacquered desk, before jumping out of her seat and pacing out of the office. Malia wasn't sure what she was supposed to do, so she followed close behind.

"Thing, thing, where can you be?" chanted Ramona, marching down the hallway. "Thing, thing, come back to me!"

Ramona Abernathy was, in a word, fancy. Today she wore a two-piece matching red pantsuit, with a patterned silk scarf wrapped around her neck. Her light brown hair was sprayed into a neat bob, with not one hair out of place. Her low-heeled shoes click-clacked on the marble floors all throughout her home, as a trail of heavy perfume hung in the air behind her.

"I just had the thing earlier, and now it has gone missing. Are you sure you haven't seen it?"

"Uh, no . . ." Malia said.

Ramona clickety-clacked into the library, another cavernous room that was lined floor to ceiling with fancy, impressive-looking leather-bound books.

"Oh, THERE it is," Ramona said, picking up what appeared to be a magnifying lens from a small side table. Malia, of course, had never laid eyes on it before. Ramona stared at her, expressionless. "Well, why are you just standing there? I'm sure there's plenty to do in the office."

"Oh, right, yes," said Malia, still stunned.

Ramona's face was something to behold, as it did not particularly move. Her eyebrows were always slightly raised, her lips drawn into a thin red line. At any given moment, it was impossible to tell if she was happy or sad or upset or angry or really experiencing any emotion at all. Right now, she looked as happy to have found the thing as she had looked unhappy to be missing it.

Malia flashed back to the time when her class had gone on a field trip to the natural history museum, and she had seen a mummy. It looked so creepy and frozen, preserved in its unnatural pose for all of time. Ramona's face reminded her a little of that.

With that beautiful thought in her mind, Malia turned and made her way back to the office. She plopped into her desk chair, exhausted.

"Did you find the thing?" Chelsea asked, never taking her eyes from her screen.

"Yes, it was in the library," said Malia.

"Great. Since that's done, I need you to replace the cartridge in the printer." Chelsea motioned to an enormous machine. It looked less like a printer and more like the commercial copy machines Malia had seen at their parents' offices.

"That's not a printer; that's, like, a house."

"Whatever. It's printing weird stripes like a zebra, and I need you to change the cartridge."

Malia sighed. She was finally used to changing diapers. She was not used to changing cartridges. However, she supposed it couldn't be any worse.

"Okay, how do I do this?" she asked.

Chelsea let out an exasperated grunt. "How am I supposed to know? Your generation is so entitled. Google it or something."

Malia grunted. How hard could this actually be? She located a door on the side of the machine, and after some pushing, a little bit of sliding, and a lot of grumbling, she got it open. The old printer cartridge was nestled safely inside. Malia grabbed it with both hands, pulling it free. Unfortunately, the cartridge had already been a bit loose, so it came out without a hitch, sending Malia flying backward.

"Arrrrrrgh!" Malia shouted as the printer cartridge exploded. A cloud of black powder landed all over her face. The more she tried to wipe it off, the more it got absolutely everywhere.

"Does this office have any paper towels?" Malia asked.

"Um, I don't know. What do you need them for?" Chelsea didn't look up.

"Chelsea."

Now Chelsea looked up. "Whoa," she said. "What happened to you?"

"The printer cartridge exploded. On my face."

"I can see that. Malia, do you have to ruin everything already? This is your first day." Chelsea opened her desk drawer and pulled out a roll of paper towels.

"Seriously? They were in your drawer this whole time?"

Malia brought the towels into the bathroom, where she

tried her best to clean the ink off her face. When she was done (or rather, when she had removed enough ink to look like she was only slightly dirty rather than like she had just escaped from a chimney), she returned to her desk, where she spent the rest of the afternoon completing a very riveting task that involved punching holes in hundreds of pages and then putting them into binders.

"My fingers are going to fall off soon," Malia said.

"Stop being dramatic," said Chelsea. "But you can probably go home now. It's almost four, and that's all we needed you to do."

This was the best news Malia had heard all day. She was expected to babysit at the Gregorys' house at five, and this would give her just enough time to run home and wash the ink off her face before heading there. (What if Connor Kelly saw her looking like a juvenile chimney sweep? The horror.) Malia gathered up her things and was just making a beeline for the exit, when a voice interrupted her.

"Where do you think you're going? I need you to do dictation."

Malia froze in her tracks. *What on earth was that?* "Dictation?" she asked.

"I need you to sit at my desk and write emails for me. I'll say them aloud, and you type them. It helps me to think."

Malia sat at the giant desk, surrounded by plaques and awards and trophies for all of Ramona's lifetime achievements. Malia glanced at the clock. This was not good. She should be on her way to the Gregory house by now.

"Dear Francine," Ramona slowly enunciated as Malia typed. Ramona cleared her throat and squinted into the air, thinking of what to say next. "I've given some thought to the endowment, and I am pleased to inform you my answer is yes."

Again, Malia checked the time. She had no idea what an endowment was, and she definitely spelled it wrong the first time, but luckily spellcheck was on her side. Ramona spoke her way through ten more emails, Malia growing more and more anxious with each one.

Had Chelsea asked her to join the team so Malia could take on all the grunt work? What had she gotten herself into? And more importantly, how would she get herself out of it?

Malia looked at her watch. Not only would she not have time to change, but now she was also officially running late for her job at the Gregorys'. By the time she pressed send on the final email, she felt like her brain was spinning. It didn't matter that she had only been an intern for one day: Malia already knew beyond a shadow of a doubt—this job was a horrible mistake.

Malia sprinted out of Ramona's impressive property down to the sidewalk. She kept right on running all the way to the Gregory house. As she approached the Gregorys' block, she didn't slow down to scan the nearby yards for Connor. For the first time ever, she didn't even care if Connor saw her racing by, looking frazzled and exhausted.

At long last, Malia arrived. But she didn't need to ring the bell, as Mrs. Gregory was already standing in the driveway, car keys in hand. All four Gregory children sat on the front steps, looking nervous.

Malia had an awful feeling in the pit of her stomach.

"I'm here! I'm so sorry!" she called.

Mrs. Gregory looked at her phone. "You're fifteen minutes late," she said. "And now I'm running late for my appointment."

Malia had never seen a client look so angry before the babysitting had even begun. She hated to let a client down, but even more, she hoped it wouldn't hurt Best Babysitters' reputation.

"I'm so sorry, Mrs. Gregory. I won't let it happen again," Malia promised.

There was a very uncomfortable pause.

"Don't," Mrs. Gregory said. With that, she got in her car and drove away.

CHAPTER SEVEN

Dot

"It can't just be any project. It has to be THE project. The project to end all projects."

Dot still hadn't come up with the idea that would win the science fair. But if there was anyone who understood, he was walking right beside her. She had managed to do some extra credit to erase her B-plus, and her science grade was back in good standing. But she still didn't know how she was going to manage to babysit and study *and* win the science fair. Especially when she didn't have a project yet.

"Let's think," said five-year-old Aloysius Blatt.

With his library of science books, table full of lab-quality experiments, extensive collection of academic medals, and graduate-level vocabulary, Aloysius was unlike any child she had ever met or really even dreamed of. He was also a handy academic resource. Last but not least, though, he was Dot's favorite babysitting charge. Today, she was taking him on a trip to the library so he could pick up a newly released book on sustainable solar technology, his latest topic du jour.

"The key, I think, is to anchor your project inside a larger issue," he said, his dark eyes shining beneath a mop of black hair. "Give it weight and meaning. Demonstrate its consequences."

Dot had a real affinity for Aloysius. It wasn't just his love of science or his advanced vocabulary that made him feel like a kindred spirit, but also their similar life circumstances. Aloysius was another only child being raised by a single mom. Now that she thought about it, he was the only other person Dot had ever met who had all these things in common.

In all of her social circles, Dot often felt like no one understood her. People liked her, sure, and they bonded over shared activities. But whenever she would visit her friends' large, colorful homes and spend time with their big, boisterous families, it often left her feeling happy in the moment, but more alone as soon as she got back home. Dot always knew that at the end of the day, she would return to her small, quiet bungalow, where there was no such thing as "family game night" because there were never enough players.

That was one of the reasons she loved babysitting Aloysius. Though he was only in kindergarten, they had some of the most enjoyable conversations she had with anyone. In Aloysius, Dot had found someone else who understood how to pass time quietly, who'd learned to find company in books and dreams and his own imagination. They'd never discussed it directly, but they didn't have to. The stories they shared, along with their comfortable silences, told her all she needed to know.

"It might be nice to do something with a far-reaching impact," Dot agreed as they came to a crosswalk. "It could be social, or environmental."

"Are there any concerns that particularly speak to you at the moment?" Aloysius asked. Dot held his hand as they crossed the street. It was always hilarious to her that Aloysius needed guidance with things like navigating traffic, yet he was able to converse better than most adults she knew.

"Bananas are disappearing, did you know that?"

"Yeah," he said. "Soon there will be no bananas."

Dot had never really been a fan of bananas, but still, it seemed like something that was worthy of attention.

"Isn't it weird to think that something could just disappear?" she said. "Especially things we've experienced in our lifetime."

"Yeah, like one day kids will go to school and learn about all these things that used to exist—rhinos, giraffes, bananas, chocolate—that aren't around anymore," said Aloysius.

"Chocolate!" Dot exclaimed. There was so much contraband chocolate hidden in her bedroom right now, safely out of view from her health-food-hoarding mother. "I can't imagine a world without chocolate." The thought was almost too much to bear.

"Climate change and weather patterns are threatening many of the things we love," said Aloysius. "Of course, the real heart of the issue—and so many other issues—is pollination."

Pollination. Something about it struck a chord.

"That's it!" Dot exclaimed. "Bees!"

"Bees?" Aloysius furrowed his brow. "Where?" He looked around, slightly panicked, as if a swarm of bees might pop out of a nearby bush.

"Bees!" she repeated. "Bees are responsible for pollination, but due to climate change, they are dying. If there are no bees, then there is no pollination. Without pollination, there is no food. Without bees, we all perish! I have to save the bees! And by saving the bees, I'd be saving the world."

Aloysius looked thoughtful for a moment. "Will you have actual bees at the fair?"

"YES!" Dot exclaimed, though she had no clue where these bees would come from. Would she need a beekeeper suit? Where would *that* come from? This was already sounding expensive.

"I'm scared of bees," he said. "But I like it. A living component! That will make for a lively and interactive display."

They were approaching the library, which was housed in an adorable brick building. The shrubs lining the front walkway had been pruned into bushy circles, like marshmallows or rabbit's tails.

Dot felt like she was on a roll. "You know, one of the main issues is that bees are highly susceptible to temperature, particularly overheating. So I just have to develop a solution to regulate the hive's temperature and ensure the bees stay cool."

Aloysius nodded his approval. "Are you thinking of a standard evaporator-compressor-condenser-expansion device?" he asked.

"You mean, like, an air conditioner?"

"Yeah."

"Precisely. A self-refrigerating hive coolant prototype." Dot loved the sound of it already.

"Sounds like a winning idea to me!" he said. "Although, you know what would be incredible?"

"What?"

"If you found a way to harness solar power to make the device entirely self-sufficient." The boy was a genius, Dot thought. Although, on second thought, she supposed he actually was.

"That would be amazing," Dot agreed.

"You know, I've been focusing a lot of my attention on sustainable solar technology," he said.

"Yes!" Dot exclaimed. She normally liked to work solo, but this project would be more complicated than anything she had taken on before. An accomplice would be a welcome addition. Especially when that accomplice was a child prodigy.

"Everyone is going to be so impressed." Aloysius beamed. "I'm going to go grab my book, but first . . ." He paused and looked down at the ground, where his little blue sneaker had come untied. Dot laughed to herself. Despite the part where he was a prodigy, Aloysius had not yet learned to tie his shoes. Dot crouched on the ground as she looped one lace around the other.

As Aloysius skipped off to find his book, Dot scanned the library. Her eyes landed on something very unsettling.

None other than Pigeon was sitting at a table, surrounded by books and an open laptop. Ugh.

Dot didn't want to interact, but it was already too late. Pigeon had seen her and waved, and it was too late to pretend she hadn't seen her. Dot begrudgingly made her way over to the table.

"Oh, hi, Dot, what brings you to the library?"

"I'm babysitting, and we came to pick up a book," Dot said, not supplying any further details.

"Babysitting? I used to babysit all the time back in New York," Pigeon said.

Dot was beginning to wonder if there was anything Pigeon didn't do. She resisted the urge to tell Pigeon she had just come from acrobatic school, just to see if Pigeon would regale her with stories of her days on the flying trapeze.

"What's all this?" Dot motioned at the piles of stuff.

"Oh, you know, since I've already gotten As in all my classes, clearly I don't need to study. So now I'm just working on some research for the science fair." Pigeon gloated. "I cannot wait."

"Oh yeah? What's your idea?"

"Of course I can't tell you that." Pigeon narrowed her beady eyes. Dot thought they reminded her of an actual pigeon. "That's confidential information."

"I'm not going to steal your idea," Dot basically scoffed. "I already have my own idea in place, and it's global in scale."

"Well, so is mine," Pigeon said.

"Great," said Dot.

"Yes, great," said Pigeon.

"Great?" Aloysius said. At some point during their exchange, he had returned from the library stacks, book in hand.

"Well, I'm excited to see how this all plays out," said Pigeon. "And of course I'm excited to see who actually wins."

"Yes. May the best woman win," said Dot.

She pivoted on one foot and booked it out of the library, knowing Aloysius was close by. She didn't want him to witness her being terse, and she couldn't stand another minute of interacting with Pigeon. Who did this person think she was, marching into this town and acting like she owned it?

"Who was that?" Aloysius asked as soon as they were out of the library.

"A person who is named after a bird," said Dot. "But nothing you need to worry about."

"Okay. Do you want to talk more about the science fair?" he asked.

"Yes!" she said. It was a very welcome change of topic.

Dot's idea was a winner. She was as good as golden.

She supposed this wouldn't be cheap to produce, but it was an investment in her future. (More so than Veronica, whose show she didn't care about. Dot was only trying to support Malia, so she supposed the concert was worth it. It's not like she wanted to see "Antisocial Media" performed live, or anything . . . Unless it was choreographed . . . And then maybe. But just a little.) If she took on some extra babysitting jobs to cover the expense and worked super hard to build it and maybe gave up a few nights' worth of sleep . . .

Dot stopped herself before she got lost in an anxious-thought spiral and breathed in for a count of four and out for a count of six, as her mom instructed during her restorative yoga class. Everything would be fine. The important thing was, she had her winning idea. Now she just had to build it. And locate an entire hive of live bees to test it out with. And figure out how to do all of this while still finding time to babysit, which was the only way she could possibly fund buying all of the necessary supplies. It all came down to logistics, really. She breathed in and out. No big deal.

CHAPTER EIGHT

MALIA

It was Friday afternoon, which meant it was time for the weekly club meeting. Every Friday after school, the girls gathered (usually at Bree's, since her room was the biggest) to discuss what had happened that week, any upcoming jobs, and other official business.

Typically, club meetings were joyous occasions. They marked the beginning of the weekend and were also just a fun time to hang out. But this week, the girls were all so busy—with school and cats and internships and extra baby-sitting jobs to raise money for concerts—the meeting almost didn't happen.

Upon arrival, all three of them flopped down on the floor, completely exhausted. They looked like a bunch of lazy sea lions, albeit in somewhat trendy clothing.

"So, McDuffin is just going to hang out everywhere, in his carrying case?" asked Malia, pointing. Two glowing eyes peered out from the middle of an angry, bald face.

"You know his name is Veronica," corrected Bree.

"He'll always be McDuffin to me," Malia said, placing her hand over her heart.

"He's, um, kind of stressed," said Bree. "He's better off in there. I'm doing you guys a favor."

She sounded more tired than Malia had ever heard her sound before. Her normally melodic voice was more of a sad croak.

"I haven't slept in a week. He's broken most of my things and even shredded the glitter chart I made to track how close we are to getting tickets. I had to hide everything else in the closet so he can't destroy it."

"I was thinking there's a lot less stuff in here than usual," Dot said, scanning the room.

Indeed, Bree's room looked less "alive" than it normally did. It was still a fitting tribute to rainbow glitter, but all of the surfaces were now cleared of their usual knickknacks. Her vanity table, usually cluttered with lip glosses and sparkly nail polishes, was entirely empty. Her desk, always covered with scented markers and rainbow glitter glue pens, had nothing on top.

"I can barely keep up with my homework, and I messed up watching Bailey after school. Veronica gets jealous and demands all my attention. I can't possibly babysit with him in the house. I tried it—just once—and Veronica ate the entire family's fish tacos and puked them into the piano."

"Oof," said Malia.

"This cat has become my full-time job!" Bree whined.

"Too bad the cat can't pay like a full-time job," Malia said.

"Do you think he'll calm down once he gets used to his environment?" asked Dot.

"Well, it's hard to say. I googled it a bunch, and some people say yes, but some people say no." Bree inhaled sharply, as if she was about to say something very important. "I've been considering taking him to a cat therapist."

"Excuse me, a WHAT?" Malia gestured wildly, prompting the caged Veronica to hiss.

"A cat therapist. Which is exactly what it sounds like. A therapist . . . for cats. Anyway, we had a phone consultation, and she said that Veronica sounds very troubled, and it would be a good idea to start seeing her on a regular basis." Bree dropped her voice to a whisper, as though whatever came next was too much for Veronica to hear. "Apparently his issues seem very deep."

Dot and Malia nodded somberly. What was there to say?

"He wrecks everything he touches. Including my happiness," Bree concluded, driving the point home. "But I love him."

"That sounds exhausting," said Malia. "And speaking of exhausting, my new internship has basically ruined my life."

"Oh no! I thought your mom said it was going to teach you invaluable lessons about business, or something," said Dot.

"No. It is an absolute nightmare," Malia said. "My job consists of doing all the horrible things Chelsea doesn't feel like doing. The only thing I'm learning is just how evil my sister really is. And it's going to take up ALL OF MY TIME. At this rate, I won't be able to buy tickets and even if I did, I probably wouldn't even have time to see the concert. This internship has eaten my life."

"Can you quit?" asked Bree.

"My mom would never allow it. And at this rate, I wouldn't even want to, because it's a matter of pride. I need to beat Chelsea at her own game. I can't give her the satisfaction of seeing me fail. I want to do such a good job that Ramona actually likes me."

"To echo what you just said, that sounds exhausting," said Dot.

"Anyway, how are things with you?" Malia asked.

"Not as bad as what you guys have going on," said Dot. "But I'm feeling super stressed about the science fair. I finally figured out my idea, which will basically save the world. It's also going to show Pigeon de Palma once and for all that I am the best at science. But it's going to take all of my energy. Not to mention a bunch of money."

"Yeah, no pressure or anything," said Malia.

"I know you can pull it off. You always do!" said Bree, her voice returning to its normal optimistic tone for first time that day.

"I hope so. I mean, I have to. It's something I've looked forward to for months and months, and now that Pigeon thinks she's some kind of competition, I have to make sure I bring my A game. It just feels like I don't have the brain space to do a good job at everything I'm supposed to be doing right now." She paused for a minute. "So actually, I was thinking. It seems like we all have so much going on. Should we put the club on hold?"

Malia gasped. The club was her baby. It was the one venture in her life that she felt good about, not to mention good at. Plus, it was her only source of cash flow. Without babysitting, how would she ever support herself, by which she meant, buy Veronica concert tickets? If the club went away, what would she be left with? Her internship. Which was even worse than being left with nothing.

"Just until things calm down?" Dot added.

"I need the money!" Bree croaked, her voice sounding very tired again. "Cat therapy is very expensive." She paused. "I also need tickets. But what will I do with cat Veronica while I'm seeing human Veronica? Can you bring a cat to a concert?"

"Stop the club?" Malia was offended. "How can you even suggest that?"

"Not forever," Dot explained. "Believe me, I need the money, too, especially with the science fair looming. Supplies are not cheap. Neither are concerts, not that I'm necessarily going. I just thought we should practice a little self-care. You know, not overload our schedules, offer ourselves a break."

"A break does sound nice . . ." Bree trailed off. For a second, it seemed like she might have fallen asleep.

Malia couldn't believe what she was hearing. The club had come so far since they started it with zero babysitting experience. They had figured out how to communicate with kids by using their intuition and only occasionally resorting to bribery. They had figured out how to attract new customers and turn them into long-term clients. They had figured out how to run a successful company and even how to fend off competition, like when Chelsea started the Seaside Sitters and tried to drive them out of business.

And that's when it occurred to her.

"Not so fast. I have an idea," Malia announced. Why hadn't she thought of it sooner? It was so obvious. "Seriously, this is going to solve everything!"

Both Bree and Dot looked afraid.

"No offense, but your plans usually mean trouble," said Dot.

"Um, yes, offense," said Malia. "Lots of offense. But also, this one is really good, I swear."

"What is it?" said Bree. She sounded excited again.

"We hire satellite babysitters." Malia paused for effect. Her friends just stared at her.

"You mean, like, employees?" asked Dot.

"Yeah, kind of. Remember that time when we tricked Chelsea into double-booking herself for two babysitting gigs, and I had to take on one of her jobs?"

"Yeah, I remember, because that was a total disaster," said Dot.

"That's because Chelsea is evil. But the idea was good. I'd take over her job, and we would divide the earnings. That's what would happen here. We find three new sitters to take our places whenever we're too busy. Then we split the earnings fifty-fifty. We can still make money, but without the stress."

"Hm. If we bring on employees, we'll have to establish payroll," said Dot.

"That sounds like a pastry. But not as much fun," said Bree.

"It's just a list of employees and how much they get paid," said Dot.

"Yeah. Not as much fun," Bree confirmed.

"And being a manager presents its own set of challenges," Dot added.

"Nah, being a boss is easy. You just act bossy," said Malia.

"How do you know?" asked Dot.

"Because I have a boss now, so I've seen firsthand how easy it is. Ramona just yells stuff out and I have to do it."

"Management is more complicated than that," Dot said. "There is a tremendous amount of psychology behind it."

"Eh, if we're paying people, I'm sure they'll be happy to do a good job. You just keep the kids relatively happy and you get money. Who wouldn't like that?" Malia was on a roll.

"But that's the point! We actually like babysitting now!" said Bree. "If we give our jobs away, won't that be sad?"

All three looked pensive for a moment.

"That's why this plan seems like the best of both worlds,"

said Malia, campaigning hard. "We're not giving up babysitting entirely. We can still take on the gigs we want, when we have the time for them. But by giving some jobs away to the new sitters, we can keep our clients, earn money, AND have time for everything else we have going on right now."

"Sounds like a win-win situation," said Dot.

Malia's phone pinged. It was a text from Ramona.

WHERE IS THE PROPOSAL FROM HAROLD DUCKMAN?

Malia was never sure if Ramona typed in all caps because she was purposefully shouting or if she just didn't know how to turn her caps lock off. Either way, it made all her communications feel that much more stressful.

To make matters worse, Malia had no idea who Harold Duckman was, never mind what the deal was with this proposal.

"So let's say I have a gig scheduled, but when I get home from school, I discover Veronica pooped on my bed and shredded my favorite pants," Bree said. "I could have one of these satellite sitters cover the job for me. And then they would still give me half of their fees?"

"Precisely," said Malia.

"LET'S DO IT!" shouted Bree.

Veronica meowed.

Malia's phone pinged again.

MEETING WITH DUCKMAN IN FIVE. ANSWER ME.

"We can hold interviews this weekend! As soon as tomorrow afternoon!" Malia said, stress creeping into her voice.

"Oh, that sounds fun!" said Bree. "How do we do it?"

"Have you ever seen those job recruitment events they have near the supermarket sometimes?" Malia asked. "It would be like that. We can put up signs and hold interviews in the gazebo. Anyone interested can come talk to us, and we pick our favorites."

"A sign! I love making signs," said Bree, coming back to life. It had been a while since Bree had made one of her signature glittery signs, Malia realized. It was nice to see a little of the old Bree spirit.

"All right. Let's meet at the gazebo tomorrow at noon," Malia said.

EARTH TO MALIA. IS YOUR PHONE BROKEN? ARE MY MESSAGES NOT GOING THROUGH?

Tomorrow couldn't come soon enough.

CHAPTER NINE

Dot

Dot loved a good professional endeavor. It was good practice for adulthood. Any chance she had to show up, look nice, and practice grown-up skills was always welcome. Secretly, she was looking forward to the interview process even more than she had ever looked forward to babysitting (unless, of course, it was for Aloysius). She'd prepared a list of interview questions, including what each candidate found interesting about babysitting, their relevant experiences, and how they might respond in an assortment of babysitting-related crises. If her experience as a sitter had taught her anything, it was that it was best to be prepared.

It felt only fitting to hold the interviews at the place where the club first came into being: the gazebo at the end of the cul-de-sac.

Dot arrived to find the gazebo decked out and ready. A banner (made by Bree) sparkled in the breeze.

WANT TO BABYSIT? INTERVIEWS TODAY! it read, in alternating rainbow glitter letters.

"I'm so excited!" said Bree.

"I just put up a bunch of flyers at the park for good measure," said Malia. "And of course, I already posted all over social."

"Does that cat have to be here?" Dot asked, gesturing toward Veronica, who sat scowling in his cat carrier. She was mostly concerned that the presence of a sneering animal made the operation seem less professional.

"Yes," said Bree. "It's safer than leaving him at home. But he's going to stay in his carrier the whole time. Just think of it like a purse."

"Your purse seems very upset," Malia said.

Sure enough, the carrier had started inching its way along the gazebo floor. Its contents appeared to be engaged in a very vicious fight with itself.

"Whoa. Are you sure he isn't going to self-destruct?" Dot looked concerned.

"It's okay," Bree sighed. "The therapist's website said I have to let him exercise his wild tendencies in order to uncover the kitten within."

"I still can't believe you're paying for that," said Malia.

"I have to," Bree whined. "It's my only hope."

The girls sat down along one side of a folding card table they had dragged over from Bree's garage. Then they waited. Nothing happened. It reminded Dot a little of when they'd first launched their babysitting website and had waited for their first calls.

"What if nobody comes?" Bree asked.

"If you build it, they will come or whatever," said Dot.

"We didn't build the gazebo," Bree said, very serious.

"But we built this organization. It's a good opportunity. People will come."

Finally, their first candidate arrived. It was none other than Pigeon de Palma. Dot noticed she was wearing the amazing boots again, but this time she had paired them with a plain black dress. She was more dressed up than Dot had ever seen her. Dot deemed the look as being appropriately—and annoyingly—professional.

"Hi, everyone! I'm very excited to be here," said Pigeon. She was so chipper and confident. "These are my references," she said, placing an enormous binder on the card table. It was even bigger than their history textbook.

"As you'll see, I have a wealth of experience babysitting. I started with my little cousins, and then sat for our neighbors back in New York. Last summer, I served as a junior au pair. I've also assisted my aunt, who is a child development psychologist. Near the back of the binder, you'll find some of the case studies I worked on with her."

Dot had to control the urge to gag.

"That's so impressive," said Malia.

Dot shot her a look. She could tell Malia was being sincere, and she did not appreciate it.

Pigeon beamed. "Back in New York, childcare was kind of my thing."

"I thought science was your thing?" Dot said. After all, wasn't that what Pigeon had just told her?

"Science is another one of my things," Pigeon said. "Also ballet. Creative writing. Singing. Classical piano . . ." She trailed off, glancing skyward as if mentally tallying the incredibly long list of her own talents. "I guess I have a lot of things," she concluded.

Veronica hissed loudly. For once, Dot thought, it seemed like he had the right idea.

"So, hypothetically, if a child you were sitting for came down with a nasty case of food poisoning under your watch, and the parents were somewhere with no reception, what would you do?" Dot asked.

"Excellent question!" said Pigeon, without skipping a beat. "The first priority is hydration. Food poisoning can come on very suddenly and be quite severe. I would make sure the child was given lots of fluids, particularly with electrolytes. The second course of action is rest. I would make the child comfortable and encourage him or her to rest. Throughout all of this, I would do my best to reassure the child that the situation was under control and continue to check that he or she didn't feel frightened or panicked."

"Hm," said Dot. This was the correct response, even if it did sound like a robot reading out of a textbook. "And, also hypothetically, if a child you were sitting for were to break a priceless object in their home, how would you manage THAT?" asked Dot, briefly flashing back to the time when one of their babysitting charges had broken a priceless golden narwhal sculpture.

"Honesty is always the best policy, in every situation, in every part of life," said Pigeon, flashing a giant smile.

UGH, thought Dot, what an insufferable know-it-all. Of

course Pigeon was right. Her answer was exactly what Dot would say when faced with the same question. But her delivery was so smug and her hair was so shiny and her smile was like something out of a beauty pageant rather than a job interview.

Dot looked to her friends for backup. Surely, Pigeon's annoyingness was universal. But to her surprise, Malia and Bree seemed to be eating it right up.

"I would be up front with the parents as soon as they returned," Pigeon continued. "And depending on the item and the circumstances around its demise, I would take full responsibility and offer to make it up to them in any way I could, whether that meant volunteering my time and services, or providing any other kind of assistance they deemed appropriate."

"I couldn't have said it better!" said Malia. She looked as if she was ready to applaud.

Bree nodded. "That's so true."

"Well, I think we've seen enough," said Dot. She didn't know about the other club members, but she was through here. It was time for Pigeon to go. "Thanks for coming."

"Thank you so much for this opportunity!" said Pigeon. "I hope to have the chance to work with you." She turned and gracefully descended the gazebo steps, her long, wavy hair glinting in the sunlight.

Next, a set of twins arrived. They looked much too young to babysit—maybe six or seven years old. Both girls wore matching black leotards, pink tights, and black tap shoes that click-clacked on the gazebo's wooden floor. Two giant black bows perched on top of their heads, polishing off the look.

"Hi!" they said in unison. It was creepy. Before Dot had a chance to ask a question or even offer them a greeting, they both said, "We're ready!"

One of them pressed a button on her phone and very loud rap music blared out of it. The twins immediately launched into a very strange though impressively complicated tap dance routine.

It went on for far too long.

As did the pause that followed.

"Wow!" said Bree. "That was, uh, dynamite!"

Malia just nodded, making the kind of face one makes when they've been given a very odd birthday present and they're not sure what it is but they have to act excited and also grateful.

"So what interests you about babysitting?" asked Dot, breaking the silence.

"Babysitting?" asked one of the twins.

"Yes, because this is an interview to become a babysitter."

"I thought this was an audition," said one twin.

"For the talent show," said the other twin.

"What talent show?" said Bree, visibly excited.

"I'm sorry for the confusion," said Malia. "But the sign clearly states that we are interviewing babysitters today." She pointed to the banner, flapping in the breeze above them.

"WE CAN'T READ YET!" yelled one of the twins, with a fury that was well beyond her years.

"Ugh. Let's GO!!" yelled the other.

And with that, they click-clacked away.

Next, a particularly rambunctious neighborhood boy arrived to threaten them with a large stick he kept calling "the sword of redemption."

"This gazebo is reserved for interviews," Dot explained.

"I'm here to take back the gazebo for my people!" he insisted, brandishing the stick until Malia finally chased him away.

The next interviewee was a girl Dot recognized from their grade, Sage Andrews. Dot didn't know much about her except that Sage had a reputation for being kind of boy crazy. She was wearing the exact same striped T-shirt as Malia but with red stripes instead of navy blue. Her hair was the same color and length as Malia's.

"Hi, there," she said, waving.

"Nice shirt," said Malia. It took Sage a second to get the joke, and then both girls laughed.

"So, um, I don't actually have any official babysitting experience. But I'm a pretty quick learner, and I think I'd be good at it," Sage offered. "To be completely honest, I didn't really like little kids very much, but then my mom's cousin came to visit from Seattle, and she has two kids who are three and five, and they were kind of fun! We read books together and stuff."

"I *completely* understand," said Malia.

"Do you have any younger siblings?" asked Bree.

"No," said Sage. "I have an older sister. Who is, like, an absolute nightmare."

"Oh my god, me too!" said Malia.

"Isn't it the worst?" said Sage.

"The worst," Malia agreed.

"Although sometimes my sister throws parties on the weekends if my parents are out of town, and a bunch of her friends come over and sometimes there are cute boys," said Sage.

"My sister wants to be a senator," said Malia matter-of-factly. "So she never does stuff like that."

Everyone nodded somberly at Malia's terrible familial luck.

"So, do you always babysit for the same families?" Sage asked.

"We have a lot of regular clients," Dot said. "And we sit for them a lot. But we're always looking to expand our business."

"Well, I would love to help out in any way I can," said Sage. "So please do keep me in mind!" She exited the gazebo with a little wave.

The boy with the stick returned for another round of terrorizing everyone. Veronica reacted particularly angrily, hissing from inside the carrier.

"There is nothing to vanquish here!" Dot grumbled, ushering the boy away. "Go take back another land."

"This is the kingdom of my people!" he insisted.

"Well, then your people can have their kingdom back in about an hour," Dot called as he trudged away.

"Boys!" said Bree, rolling her eyes.

As if on cue, a spacey boy wandered into the gazebo. He seemed like he might be lost. He wore an oversize T-shirt and baggy jeans, and moved at a snail's pace, as though he was taking a slow, leisurely stroll on a tropical beach rather than encountering a panel of highly judgmental girls.

"Hi there, can we help you with something?" Bree asked.

"Heyyyyyyy," he said. He had an alarmingly chill vibe, as

evidenced by the way he dragged his syllables out for much longer than was necessary.

"Are you guys selling Girl Scout cookies or something?"

"No. We're holding an open call for our babysitting organization," said Dot. "Did nobody read the signage?"

"Aww, too bad. I love cookies," he said.

"They're great!" Bree agreed.

"So you guys, like, need someone to babysit you?"

"No, we *are* babysitters," Dot corrected. "And we are looking to hire more sitters, to come work for our company."

"That's so coooooool," he said, in his slow, sleepy drawl. "I would, like, do that."

"Well, we're only looking for candidates with experience—" Dot began.

"Hey, kitty, kitty," the boy said, noticing Veronica. "Who's this?"

"That's Veronica," said Malia.

"Don't talk to him—he's bats!" warned Dot.

"Sweeeeet name. Hi there, Veronica. My name is Brody," he said, bending down to open the cat carrier.

"Don't do that!" screeched all three girls at once, but it was too late. The carrier was already open. They braced themselves for the bedlam that was about to unfold. But to everyone's surprise, Brody scooped Veronica out of the case, and he immediately curled up oh-so-sweetly in Brody's arms. "Hey, fella, you're such a nice cat."

The girls sat there, utterly dumbfounded, while Brody petted a very chill animal that in no way resembled Veronica. Was he a cat whisperer? What on earth was going on?

"When can you start?" asked Bree.

"She means *hypothetically*, if you were hired, when would you be available to start?" corrected Dot.

"Like, totally. Yeah," said Brody. "I can start now."

For the first time maybe ever, Veronica purred.

CHAPTER TEN

Bree

Well, we have to hire Brody, because he's a wizard," said Bree as she folded up the glittery sign.

Bree had never been more certain about anything in her entire life, except of course her decision to adopt Veronica. Though, in hindsight, adopting Veronica turned out to be far more drama than she'd ever anticipated. But whatever! Brody was magic. There was no reason to doubt it.

"I agree with that," said Malia.

"But he didn't even know this was an interview. And he's never babysat before," said Dot.

Dot was so practical. Bree had no idea what it must be like to think like Dot.

"Yeah, but neither had you until pretty recently," argued Malia. "And now you're pretty good at it."

"And also? Wizard," added Bree. "You saw the way he hyp-notized the cat. Imagine what he could do with a child."

Dot backed down. "Fine. As long as he passes the training."

"Obviously. Everyone needs to pass the training." Malia looked down at her notebook. "Pigeon is, like, a professional babysitter, so obviously we have to hire her."

"Ugh, her level of preparation was borderline ridiculous," said Dot.

"But she seems good at so many things," said Bree. She knew that Dot wasn't a fan of Pigeon, but her interview had been so inspiring. Bree wanted to be good at that many things. Or even half as many things. Even, like, two more things would be an improvement.

"But what about the binder? And the research on child psychology? That was so unnecessary." Dot crossed her freckly arms.

"Yeah, she kind of has a stressful vibe," Malia agreed. "She's a classic overachiever. Like someone else I know."

"What? Me?" Dot acted insulted, though it was obvious she kind of liked being called an overachiever. "I am not like Pigeon. Are you insinuating I'm that smug?"

"No, but you are an overachiever . . ."

"Guilty as charged." Dot held up her hands in a show of surrender. "But what should we do? You know how I feel about Pigeon, but I'll admit it might not be the worst thing to let her take over some of our work." Plus, Dot secretly thought to herself, if Pigeon was super busy babysitting, she'd have less time to devote to the science fair, which was an added benefit for Dot.

"So let's hire her," said Bree, who was keeping one eye on Veronica. He was watching a fly buzzing right outside his carrier. With every passing moment, he grew increasingly angry that he couldn't escape in order to hunt it. Bree felt guilty at his obvious discomfort. She wanted him to be happy, but she also wanted herself to be happy. Pet ownership was so hard.

"I got a really good feeling about Sage," said Dot.

"Me too!" said Bree. "She seems really kind. And like she has good instincts."

"And an incredible fashion sense," Malia cut in.

"And so much of babysitting is about intuition over experience," Dot argued. "So I vote for Sage."

"Are we afraid that maybe she's a little too boy crazy?" Malia asked.

Her friends gave her confused looks.

"What does that have to do with babysitting?" Bree asked.

"I don't know, maybe it would distract her from giving all her attention to the kids or something."

"Oh, you're one to talk. You spend the entire time at the Gregory house trying to peek over the fence at Connor," said Dot.

"And sometimes you'll also watch for him out the window," Bree added.

"Only when coming or going," Malia said, defensively.

"Okay. So our options are Brody, Pigeon, and Sage," said Dot.

"What are the next steps?" asked Bree. She was so proud of everyone, expanding their club and being all professional and stuff. This was a big step for them. The thought of having six babysitters made her want to cry a little. (In a good way.)

"We let each of our candidates know they've been chosen," said Dot.

"I can do that now!" said Malia, reaching for her phone. "I'll also invite them to the park for a group training day tomorrow."

"Training day? Tomorrow? That's a lot of curriculum to develop in one day," Dot said, visibly stressed. She'd mentioned earlier that she wanted to spend the day working on her project and prepping for an upcoming test. "We have to cover the basics, safety protocol, hygiene, ethics . . ."

"Nah," said Malia. "I think we just throw a bunch of challenges at them all at once. After all, isn't that how we learned?"

Everyone nodded.

"It's true," Dot agreed. "We had zero experience, and Mrs. Woo just let us into her home and let us watch her children, like trial by fire. And we figured it out."

"You know how Coach K makes the soccer team do a bunch of crazy drills that are more intense than anything they'd ever encounter in an actual game?" Malia said. "Then, when game time comes, it seems like a breeze. I say we do the same thing with the new sitters."

"I like it," said Dot.

Bree's eyes lit up. This was sounding like a lot of fun. "We should set up an obstacle course and recreate different situations that they might run into while babysitting! And maybe some situations they probably wouldn't run into that might be fun anyway!"

"Yeah!" said Malia.

"And I can play a baby!" Bree added.

If she was being honest, Bree was mostly excited about getting to play a baby.

"YES!" said Malia.

"Ooh! We should have a hiring ceremony," said Bree. She loved ceremonies. They were almost as much fun as parties. Especially if they involved a gong. She didn't know where she could get a gong, but she would look for something equally loud in her family's garage.

"Ooh, an initiation. That could be good," added Dot.

"With cookies! And a secret handshake or something," said Bree. "I can take care of that part." Now she was really excited.

"Congratulations, partners," said Malia. She extended her hand, prompting Bree and Dot to place their hands on top.

"To our very first expansion!" said Dot.

CHAPTER ELEVEN

MALIA

"**W**here did Bree get a megaphone?" Malia asked.

Dot just shrugged.

The newly expanded club, including Pigeon, Brody, and Sage, had gathered in the grassy area behind the gazebo, where the hiring ceremony was officially underway. Bree had appointed herself the grand master of ceremonies. Malia was proud to be the CEO, but acting like a cheerleader was way more of Bree's thing, so Malia was happy to let her have this. Megaphone in hand, Bree paced back and forth on the raised platform that led to the monkey bars, while the rest of the group sat on the grass below her, ever the captive audience. Slightly removed from the crew, Veronica looked on from his cat carrier, scowling over the proceedings.

"Welcome to the next chapter of your life!" Bree shouted, flashing everyone her brightest smile.

She sounded like she was channeling one of the super-high-energy self-help gurus from the videos Chelsea would sometimes watch on YouTube. Malia couldn't help but wonder where on earth she was getting this stuff from. It was a new side of Bree (though, given her enthusiasm for everything, it wasn't particularly surprising).

"Are you ready to watch some children?" Bree yelled. "Who's ready to watch some children? Let me see a show of hands!"

The new hires put their hands in the air. They seemed pretty jazzed, but it was also possible they were just being polite.

"Woooooooo!" Bree shouted at the top of her lungs.

"How long do we let this go on for?" Dot asked Malia.

"I don't know, another minute maybe?" Malia guessed.

Now Bree was stomping her feet, creating a complicated rhythm.

"When I say 'baby,' you say 'sit'!" she chanted, really getting into it. "Baby!"

"Sit?" Pigeon, Brody, and Sage gave their tentative reply.

"That's it! Now louder!" she hollered. "Baby!"

"Sit!"

"Baby!"

"Sit!"

With one final "Woooo!" Bree hopped off the platform. As promised, she ended the ceremony by passing around a tin of assorted cookies.

"Do these have gluten in them?" asked Pigeon.

"Yeah," said Dot, before adding, "because gluten is delicious."

As everyone but Pigeon munched on their cookies, Malia handed each new sitter a giant plastic rain poncho.

"Sweeeeeet," said Brody.

"What do we need these for?" asked Sage.

"Oh, you'll see," said Malia with a laugh. "Babysitting is not for the faint of heart."

"Here we have an obstacle course." Dot motioned to the complicated setup stretching across the lawn.

The girls had created a special path that snaked all over the park, with arrows pointing the way. It started at the jungle gym, which they had decked out with streamers, then led to a "scary passageway" made of Hula-Hoops and a sheet printed with cartoon animals parading across it. At one particularly challenging part of the course, there was an old Slip 'N

Slide, followed by a "moat" (actually a kiddie pool filled with Kool-Aid).

"As you make your way through the maze, some unforeseen challenges will pop up, just as they do when babysitting," Malia said. "Trust your instincts. Do your best to keep calm and continue moving forward."

"One more thing," said Dot, handing each sitter a wrapped parcel. "You must carry this sack of flour, which is approximately the weight of one baby, the entire time. If you drop it, you will be disqualified."

"Whoa," said Sage.

"Awesome," said Brody.

"No problem!" said Pigeon.

"On your mark!" Bree yelled into the megaphone. She was really enjoying this whole megaphone thing, Malia thought. "Get set!" Bree yelled, pausing for effect before concluding, "GO!"

The new hires were off, scrambling up the rope ladder that led to the upper level of the jungle gym. Pigeon was leading the pack, but Sage was giving her a pretty good run for her money. Brody, several paces behind them, looked like he was moving peacefully through a pool full of molasses.

They swung across the monkey bars, sacks of flour tucked

ingeniously into wherever their shirts and pants would allow. They slid down the slide and sprinted on to the next part of the course. Well, Sage and Pigeon sprinted. Brody pretty much strolled.

Malia wasn't yet sure what to make of the new hires. She was wary of their performance. Did Brody have no sense of urgency? Had Sage never encountered a child before? But she wanted this plan to work. So she tried to remain optimistic.

"Uh-oh! You're approaching the moat!" Malia called as the hires inched closer to the strange homemade structures, including the pool of Kool-Aid. "But instead of a dragon, this moat is being guarded by a giant baby!"

Bree, wearing Veronica's glittery blue bonnet, toddled around, acting like a giant baby.

"Waaaaah!" she yelled. "I'm a baby!"

She weaved her way in and out of the course, trying to distract and confuse everyone.

"Wait, what's going on?" Pigeon said.

"GIVE ME MY TOY!!!" Bree screamed, three inches away from Pigeon's ear.

"What? What toy?" Pigeon asked, confused.

Bree fell to the ground and began pulling on Pigeon's leg, the way so many children had done to her in the past month.

"LADY! YOU. HAVE. MY. TOY!!!!!!!!!!!!!" Bree seemed to be enjoying herself a little too much.

"I don't have a toy!" Pigeon said helplessly.

Brody looked on with a confused expression. Sage just laughed.

"The point," Dot calmly explained from the sidelines, "is that sometimes a child will make a demand that doesn't make any sense."

"They might think your earrings are a toy. Or your hair. Or they might be referring to some imaginary toy, just to be annoying," Malia added.

"The point of this exercise is, when a child becomes stressful, how well do you deal with it?" said Dot.

"GIVE ME MY TOY!" Bree shouted. Now she was also kicking and screaming while rolling on the ground. It was really an epic tantrum.

"Yo, kid. Chill," said Brody. "You can totally have your toy."

"I'm a baby!" Bree screamed. "Give me attention!"

"Babies do not act like this," said Pigeon. "This one is speaking in full sentences."

"WAAAAAAAAAAH!" yelled Bree. This time, she sounded a lot like a baby.

"Hi there, baby," said Sage, in a googly voice. Malia admired how willing she was to go along with the challenge. Were their roles reversed, Malia wasn't sure she would be as good of a sport. "Don't cry!" Sage knelt down so she was on Bree's level. She tickled Bree under the chin, which looked ridiculous, since Bree wasn't actually a baby. But Bree just smiled.

The trainees continued to the next part of the course, crawling through the makeshift tunnel. As they emerged from the tunnel, another surprise was waiting.

"Uh-oh! Look out!" Bree yelled as she started throwing mud all over them.

Pigeon shrieked as the mud slid off her plastic poncho.

"Dirt is a big part of the job!" Dot said gleefully.

"Baby diarrhea is real!" yelled Malia. "You need to get used to it!"

"I'm a baby! I made a mess!" Bree yelled. "Clean it up!" She kept throwing mud at them.

Muddied and mystified, the junior babysitters soldiered on.

"Whoaaaaaaa," said Sage, sliding on a patch of mud. "Help!" she called as she careened toward Pigeon. But instead of helping, Pigeon ducked out of the way. Now Sage was headed right for the Kool-Aid pool. The babysitters winced, preparing for the inevitable Kool-Aid tsunami once Sage crashed with the water. But instead, she screeched to a halt at the last moment. She looked back at the other sitters.

"Are we done now?" she asked.

"Okay. That was . . . interesting," said Malia.

"The good news is, all of you are still holding your flour babies, and all of you passed," Dot announced.

The new hires gave each other high fives.

"Congratulations!" Bree cheered. "Now, you may each receive your official club hat."

"Our what?" Pigeon asked.

Bree retrieved a garbage bag from beneath a nearby tree and proceeded to pull three glittery top hats from it.

"Aren't those left over from last New Year's Eve?" Malia asked.

Bree shot her a look. "No, these are the *official babysitting hats*," Bree said, handing a sparkly pink hat to Brody.

"Sweeeeeeet," he said, placing the hat immediately upon his head.

"Do we have to, like, wear these when we babysit?" Pigeon asked, accepting a sparkly lavender hat.

"Are there any boys around?" Sage asked, glancing from side to side.

"Boys LOVE sparkles," Bree said, handing Sage the remaining silver hat. "Everyone does."

"Congratulations, everyone! This means you're ready for the next round of training," Malia continued, inspiring a look of concern to spread across each of their faces. "With real live kids."

CHAPTER TWELVE

Bree

"O h my!" said Mrs. Woo when she saw that six sitters had arrived to watch her two young daughters. "This is quite the collective."

"PARTYYYYYY!" yelled five-year-old Ruby at the sight of the whole gang.

It was, Bree had to admit, an awful lot of people.

"We're excited to announce that we're expanding our business," Dot said. "And as one of our most valued clients, we wanted our new hires to meet your girls right away so everyone can get comfortable and acquainted."

"How nice. Well, help yourselves to the snacks, as usual," said Mrs. Woo, putting her keys into her purse before adding, "I just hope there are enough of them!"

As soon as their mother's car backed away, the Woo girls,

five-year-old Ruby and three-year-old Jemima, exploded like little human fireworks.

"WE'RE FREE!" sang Ruby, running into the living room.

"FEE! FEE!" yelled Jemima, close behind.

"THE OGRE HAS LEFT THE BUILDING!" Ruby continued yelling. "THE DRAGON HAS LEFT THE MOAT! THE TROLL HAS LEFT THE BRIDGE!"

The new sitters looked the way Bree had felt the first time Veronica peed on one of her jackets. Very confused, a little bit worried, but mostly not sure how to fix it.

"Don't worry," Bree whispered. "They calm down eventually."

"IT'S MY PARTY AND I'LL CRY IF I WANT TO," sang Ruby, jumping up and down on a living room chair.

"CWY IF I WANT TO!" added Jemima.

"Girls! There is to be no jumping on furniture," said Malia.

"But it's my party!" said Ruby.

"Parties are meant to be fun, not destructive," said Dot.

"Depends on the party." Ruby narrowed her eyes.

"Let's all sit in a circle so we can get to know our new friends," Bree suggested.

Ruby put her hands on her hips, deciding whether or not to fall for this.

"OHHHHHH-kay," she said, reluctantly sitting down. "But this doesn't look like any party I've ever been to."

Everyone sat in down in the Woos' living room. They were all spread out across the couch, the chairs, and the floor, but everyone could see everyone else, and that's what was important. Everything in the room—the couch, the carpet, the bookshelves, the curtains—was white, which never failed to make Bree nervous.

"Pigeon, Brody, and Sage, meet Ruby and Jemima," said Malia.

"Hi, everyone!" said Pigeon. "It's so lovely to meet you."

Bree noticed that Pigeon had pulled a notebook out of her bag and was taking notes.

"Hey," said Sage. She seemed nervous.

"Yo." Brody offered a little wave.

"Hewwo!" said three-year-old Jemima.

"Hi. I am Ruby and I am five and this is my house. I like ice cream and also the color purple and also the movie *Moana* and also rabbits and yesterday my mom said that if I practice the piano every day for a month she'll buy me a scooter and I asked if it could be a scooter with streamers on the handles and she said yes and I think they should be purple streamers but maybe they should be silver streamers what do you think?" Ruby said, in a single breath.

"Silver streamers sound pretty great to me," said Pigeon.

"So! What does everyone feel like doing today?" Bree asked. She hoped someone would suggest a board game or a movie or some other relatively low-key activity.

"I WANNA PLAY SCARY CLOWN!" yelled Ruby.

"How does that work?" asked Brody.

"I scare you!" Ruby explained matter-of-factly. "And then, while you're still scared, I yell, 'SCARY CLOWN! SCARY CLOWN!'" She collapsed into a fit of giggles.

"SCAWY! SCAWY CWOWN!" added Jemima. She nodded her head so intensely that her tiny ponytail continued to bobble on top of her head for a few seconds afterward.

"That sounds like . . . not a good idea," said Dot.

Bree had to agree. Although she liked almost everything in the universe, Bree was very anti-clown. Her stepdad, Marc, had once hired a clown for her birthday party, and she had never really recovered.

"Hide-and-go-seek?" Ruby suggested innocently.

Bree remembered when Ruby had pulled that stunt the very first time the girls babysat them. The Woo kids had hidden so well, everyone thought they were kidnapped and lost forever.

"And again . . . not a good idea." Dot thought for a minute. "How about we all play a nice, quiet game together? So we can get to know our new friends."

"SCAWY CWOWN?" Jemima asked at a very high volume.

"No, like a calm game," said Bree. "Like I Spy. Does everyone know how that works?"

Jemima shook her head no.

"I look around the room and pick something that I see," Bree explained, "But I don't tell anyone what it is. Instead I give you clues, like 'I spy with my little eye, something big.' And then you have to guess what I'm seeing."

"I spy Dot!" said Ruby. "I spy Malia! I spy a boy and I forget what his name is!"

"My name is Brody."

"Not quite!" said Bree. "You don't tell us what you spy, you just give us a hint."

Ruby looked at her quizzically.

"I'll go first so everyone can see how it works," said Pigeon.

Dot sort of grunted. Bree couldn't be sure, but she thought it was on purpose.

"I spy . . . with my little eye . . . something green!"

"The plant! The plant!" yelled Ruby.

It was the only green thing in the entire room.

"Correct!" said Pigeon. "That was great!"

Ruby clapped with glee.

"I'll go next!" said Sage. "I spy with my little eye . . . something white!"

Bree gasped. This was a tricky one. Almost every single thing in the room was white! How was anyone supposed to get this?

"Couch!" yelled Ruby.

"Nope," said Sage.

"Vase!" yelled Ruby.

"Nope," said Sage.

It went on like this for a while, with Ruby guessing every last item in the room. All of them were wrong. Bree had no idea what it could be.

"WHAT IS IT?" Ruby yelled, enraged.

"It's the wall!" said Sage.

Sage seemed proud of herself for stumping a small child, but Ruby was not amused.

"The WALL? The WALL?" She gripped her cheeks with

her fingers and pulled on them, making a silly goon face. "THAT'S NOT FAIR! You can't guess the *wall*."

"Of course it's fair," said Sage. "You're just supposed to guess something you see."

"UGH! WHATEVER. I have to go to the bathroom!" Ruby said suddenly. "Excuse me." And with that, she dramatically exited the room.

"This is fun!" said Sage, as though she had actually expected small children to be terrible and was happily surprised with the experience.

"I have a few questions," said Pigeon in a scholarly tone.

"Mm-hmm?" said Dot.

"Do the parents ever spell out any restrictions? Do you have any clients who have special dietary needs, or allergies?" asked Pigeon, scribbling in her notebook.

"Usually, if there is anything you need to know, the parents will tell you up front," said Malia.

"But of course it's always a good idea to ask when you're sitting for someone for the first time," said Dot. "I always ask about any special needs when I'm getting the emergency contact info."

"Right, yes, of course." Pigeon scribbled away.

Suddenly, Ruby popped up from behind the couch, banging a pot with a wooden spoon.

Pigeon screamed and jumped three feet in the air.

"SCARY CLOWN! SCARY CLOWN!" Ruby dissolved into a fit of giggles.

She and Jemima both rolled on the floor, basically combusting with laughter.

"We towed you we wanna play scawy cwown," said Jemima, as if that were an acceptable explanation.

"Why was I the only one who got scared by that?" said Pigeon. She pointed at the other sitters. "You guys didn't even jump."

"Eh, I kinda figured something like that would happen," said Malia with a shrug.

It was true. With the Woo girls, you never could tell what they'd do next, so it was best to expect anything.

"Don't worry," said Bree in an encouraging tone. "You'll get the hang of it."

Bree hoped she was right about this, but she wasn't so sure. They were counting on the new sitters to make everything work. It was a matter of earning money for the Veronica concert tickets, and supplies for the science fair, and visits to the pet psychologist, but even more, it was about sanity. There was a lovely but psycho kitty that needed all her time and attention. These sitters were their only hope.

She looked into each of their eyes, so worried but so hopeful.

They would totally figure it out . . . right?

CHAPTER THIRTEEN

MALIA

Where is the key?

Malia read the text and let out a sigh. Was Sage for real?

What key? she texted back.

To get in the front door! Sage typed.

There is no key, Malia responded. The parents won't leave until you arrive. Just ring the doorbell.

This was absurd. It reminded Malia of a thing her dad often said: common sense is not so common.

Today was Sage's first solo babysitting job, for the three youngest Gregory kids, and so far she wasn't inspiring the greatest confidence. She had already texted Malia multiple times to confirm the time, the address, and the children's names. Now, apparently, entering the house was also proving to be difficult.

Malia was concerned. This was basic, basic stuff. Plus, they had covered it in training. Malia didn't have time for this. She had an internship to attend to. Was Sage a space cadet or were her nerves just getting the best of her? Malia could only hope she would get it together soon. The reputation of the club was on the line. Not to mention the fate of her relationship with Connor. They were only a few extra babysitting jobs away from having the funds to see Veronica—unless, of course, Sage got everyone fired.

"MALIA! I need you to alphabetize something," Ramona called, jolting Malia back to the present.

"Coming!" she said, scurrying into Ramona's office.

"I have this pile of invoices," Ramona said, motioning to what could more appropriately be characterized as a landslide of paper. "I need you to file them, in alphabetical order, and in the appropriate categories, of course."

Malia started to scoop the enormous pile of paper into her arms.

"Also, you'll notice multiple invoices have sticky notes on them. In each case, something needs to be done before you file it. Sometimes you'll have to write an email. Other times you'll have to double check an amount or make a photocopy and mail it . . . you get the point. Use your best judgment and ask me if you have any questions."

Just as she got back to her desk, Malia's phone pinged. Another text from Sage.

Can the kids watch TV?

Yes.

Thought so. But how do I turn it on?

Certainly this was a joke.

Malia settled in and started on the invoices. She had only filed one (a bill from Ramona's cleaning service) when her phone pinged again. *Well, whaddaya know,* she thought. Another text from Sage.

Do you happen to know the Wi-Fi password?

All the important info is on the fridge.

"What does she think I am — Google?" Malia said under her breath.

"Who — Ramona?" Chelsea asked.

"No, never mind."

She had only filed two more invoices when her phone pinged yet again. At this point, Malia was expecting it.

The twins are crying. What do I do?

Why are they crying?

Of course, now that it was important, talkative Sage stopped answering. Malia watched her phone obsessively, hoping to see something—anything—mildly reassuring pop up. But nothing did. A few more highly distracted minutes ticked by.

Everything okay over there? Malia asked.

No answer.

Just let me know that it's under control.

Silence. A few minutes passed.

Let me know if you need backup.

Still no answer.

Malia filed another invoice, likely under the incorrect letter. Now she was in a panic. What was going on over there? This was the club's reputation on the line. Not to mention the children's safety.

Malia tried actually calling Sage, like it was an old movie or something.

The phone rang and rang, but nobody answered.

Even more panicked, Malia grabbed her bag.

"What are you doing?" Chelsea said.

"I'm just going to check on something. I'll be right back."

"Going to check on what?" Chelsea asked, but Malia was already on her way out the door.

She raced all the way to the Gregorys' house. For the first time ever, she hoped Connor Kelly wouldn't be anywhere on his family's property, because she couldn't afford to stop and talk to him.

As she rushed up the Kellys' front walk, her panic grew. The smell was unmistakable. It was smoke . . . and it was coming from the Gregory house.

Malia sprinted through the front door, ready to encounter a true disaster. Instead she saw Sage, along with Jonah, Plum, and Piper, roasting marshmallows around the gas-powered fireplace.

"What is going on here?" Malia spat.

"Oh, hi, Malia! What a surprise!" said Sage.

"MAWIA!" said Jonah, toddling over to hug her leg.

"You weren't answering my messages," Malia said. She was surprised by how much her tone sounded like that of a parent. "I thought something was wrong. And then, on my way over, I smelled smoke."

"Oh! I just didn't want to bother you anymore," said Sage.

Like you didn't already bother me enough, thought Malia.

"We're having a great time. Plum and Piper said they always roast marshmallows with their parents on movie night, so we thought it might be a fun thing to re-create during the day!"

Before Malia even had a chance to respond, her phone pinged. What was it with this day?

WHERE ARE YOU?

This time it was Ramona.

Just running an errand. Be right back!

Malia typed in lower-case letters, hoping Ramona might realize how regular people text.

I DON'T RECALL ASKING YOU TO RUN AN ERRAND.

Malia sighed. No such luck.

Malia didn't know how to respond. She reasoned her best course of action was to run back to the office while Ramona was still waiting for a response.

"Okay, I have to go. But please keep me posted and feel free to text me if—" Malia hadn't even finished her sentence when her phone pinged again.

I SEE A LOT OF INVOICES STILL ON YOUR DESK. I EXPECT YOU'LL FIN- ISH WITHIN THE HOUR? HAVE ANOTHER TASK FOR YOU.

"Bye!" Malia yelled, booking it out of the Gregory house. When she had suggested hiring satellite sitters, this definitely wasn't how she imagined it going. In its own way, being a boss felt like more work than just being an employee. Her phone pinged again as she raced down the front walk.

P.S. NOT HAPPY

How was it possible that she felt even more stressed than before? And also, somehow, like she was letting everyone down?

"Hey, Malia," said a nearby bush. It wasn't just any voice. It was THE voice. Malia stopped in her tracks.

Connor's head popped up from behind the offending shrub. He held up the Frisbee that he had apparently been rummaging for.

"Hi, Connor," Malia said.

"Me and Aiden were just about to play a game of Frisbee," said Connor. "Do you want to join?"

Malia's heart stopped. This was the moment she had been waiting for. That is, this was the moment she had been waiting for *before she was employed*. Because then she could have taken advantage of it.

CRUEL UNIVERSE, thought Malia. Was this some kind of horrible joke? She had been waiting days, months—maybe her whole life—for this exact opportunity and now she had to turn it down to go file some invoices for a lunatic.

"I'd love to. But I have to go back to my internship," Malia said, hoping it at least made her sound professional and impressive.

But Connor just shrugged.

"Too bad," he said. "Okay." And then he loped off, into his backyard, where all of Malia's dreams were about to come true without her.

CHAPTER FOURTEEN

Dot

Dot supposed that saving the world wasn't meant to be easy. She supposed that Albert Einstein and Marie Curie and Sir Isaac Newton and Benjamin Banneker and Bill Gates and Sally Ride and Mae Jemison and Thomas Edison and Galileo had all encountered their fair share of setbacks.

Still, she had expected winning the science fair to be a little easier than this. And she was annoyed.

"Bee AC!" she addressed the tiny contraption on top of her desk. "What is wrong with you? What am I not doing right?"

The miniature self-refrigerating hive coolant device was presenting more challenges than she had originally anticipated. First, there was the issue of the size. She was working on a pretty small scale, which called for tremendous attention to detail, and also put a strain on her eyes. It was adorable, but that wasn't the point. It needed to be functional, too.

Then there was the issue of pressure. Not the air pressure, which she actually had a pretty good grip on, but the emotional pressure. Dot normally felt like things came easy to her, especially when it came to grades and school. This struggling feeling was both unfamiliar and unwelcome. Winning the science fair—and saving the world—was something she'd been working toward her entire life. Everything needed to be perfect. Better than perfect, even.

Does he talk?

Dot's phone lit up with a text from Pigeon. Today was her first time babysitting Aloysius, and as was his way when around new people, he was entirely mute.

Yes. He just takes a while to open up, Dot responded. Be patient.

Dot wished she could be the one spending the afternoon with Aloysius. She thought back to the first time the club ever watched him and how he had refused to speak. Dot remembered how strange the other sitters had found it, but she understood. Sometimes it wasn't easy to open up to new people. Sometimes it felt better to observe for a while until you were comfortable.

"Is that your problem?" she asked the tiny air conditioner. "Are you just not comfortable yet?"

Using a tweezer, Dot moved the tiny metal conductor so it covered a greater surface area of the parts it was meant to connect. Suddenly, the machine came to life.

"IT WORKS!" she yelled, to no one. "OMIGOD OMIGOD IT WORKS!"

It was so beautiful. She wanted to watch it all day, marveling at the wonder she had created. She wondered if this is what it felt like to have a child.

Then Dot's phone lit up, drawing her attention to the other side of her desk. Another message from Pigeon.

What should I ask him? Help me.

Dot didn't mind answering; she wanted to be helpful. Part of her didn't necessarily want Pigeon to succeed, but she hated the idea of Aloysius being uncomfortable. Plus, deep down, her competitive side relished being able to give Pigeon the answers for once.

Dot typed quickly, her fingers flying rapidly across the phone's surface. She couldn't risk taking her eye off her device for more than a few moments.

Are you in his room? If not, go there, and use something he's working on as a visual reference. He's always working on a bunch of projects and loves to talk about them.

Dot had barely typed the message out when she was interrupted by a loud sound.

Ker-flume!

Dot looked up from her phone to see the bee AC going up in smoke.

She gasped. Her heart sank.

"It that smoke?" Dot's mom appeared at the doorway, carrying a large pink orb. She was her unique mixture of alarmed and Zen.

"My invention," Dot said, pointing one shaking finger at the desk. "It's . . ." She was so choked up she could barely make words. "It's dead."

Dot's mom entered the room, her long purple robe trailing behind her.

"Who's dead?"

"My science project. It must have overheated. I don't even know what happened. I wasn't looking at it, and the next thing I know, POOF!" She closed her eyes, afraid that if she looked at the smoking device for one second longer, she might cry.

"Oh, Dot, I'm sorry." Her mother looked dismayed. Then a thought danced across her face. "Here, hold this." Dot's mom handed her the pink ball. It weighed about a million pounds. "Rose quartz is a healing stone. I was just doing a meditation with it for that very purpose."

"Um, okay," Dot said.

"I'm going to get something, I'll be right back."

Her mom flounced away, leaving Dot alone.

How had this happened?

Dot stood there, holding a pink crystal ball, watching her dreams quite literally go up in smoke. It might have been funny if it wasn't so sad.

Her mom burst back into the room.

"You know, your Saturn is currently in Sagittarius," she said. Like that was a reasonable explanation.

"What on earth does that mean?"

"It means that right now is a time of many lessons, but also that projects may not go the way you anticipate," her mom explained. "But try to use this as an opportunity for personal growth."

"I see. I will take that under advisement."

Her mom took the pink orb back and handed Dot a small, metallic stone.

"Take this. It's pyrite. It will help you stay motivated and to harness your power."

Dot looked down at her palm, where the pyrite shone in the light.

"Thanks," said Dot. She didn't believe this rock had the power to bring her any closer to a science fair victory, but she had to admit, it was rather pretty. She figured the least she could do was carry it. At this rate, it probably couldn't hurt.

Dot hoped everything was going slightly better with Pigeon. She would need her half of Pigeon's babysitting fees — and fast — to replace the melted prototype parts.

As if on cue, another text popped up:

Thanks! It worked. He's showing me his latest research.

Good, Dot thought, running her thumb over the pyrite. At least today wasn't a total disaster.

CHAPTER FIFTEEN

MALIA

Once again, it was time for the weekly club meeting. Malia arrived at Bree's room to find Dot already spread out on the floor, eating what appeared to be an entire candy store.

"I'm stress eating," she said when she saw Malia's expression. "My science fair project is a total disaster and you know the only thing my mom stocks is organic twig bites, so I can't get any good stress eating done at home."

"Where's Bree?" Malia asked.

"Don't ask," said Dot.

A few seconds later, Bree entered the room, holding a wadded-up bath towel. Her clothes were wet, and she looked exhausted.

"Hi, guys," she said, shutting the door behind her.

As soon as the door was locked, she put the towel on the ground and out popped a particularly psychotic Veronica. His eyes glowed neon. He was so angry that the wrinkles on his face were actually moving.

"Mrrreow!" he screeched, bounding all around the room as if he were on fire.

"I had to give him a bath," explained Bree. "I have to give him a bath once a week."

"And clearly he enjoys that," said Malia, her voice dripping with sarcasm.

"Cats hate water," Bree said. "Even sane cats with the ability to like other stuff. So you can imagine how he feels about it."

"Sounds fun," said Dot, shoveling gummy bears into her mouth as though they were popcorn.

Bree plopped down next to her friends.

"My back hurts," she said. "My whole life hurts."

"I feel that," said Malia.

"The good news is, the new babysitters haven't killed anyone yet," said Dot.

"Yeah, speaking of babysitters, should we figure out the schedule for this coming week?" Malia asked. As soon as she said it, she realized how much she had missed feeling like she was in charge — in charge of the club, in charge of a child, in charge of anything.

The girls pulled out their phones to cross-check what they had booked.

"Okay, so the satellite sitters have already taken on three jobs and so far they haven't totally ruined anything," Malia said.

"So we're only six jobs away from the Veronica tickets," said Dot, quickly adding, "Not that I care about that. But I know how important it is for you guys."

Malia continued. "The Gregory kids need a sitter on Tuesday evening and again on Saturday afternoon. I have my internship on both of those days, so I was going to put Sage on that." She supposed this meant it would be another week without additional Connor sightings.

"I'm totally slammed with my project, so Pigeon is covering for Aloysius pretty much every day after school, except for Friday, when he has a mini MENSA meeting," Dot added. At this point, she had completely finished the gummy bears and already moved on to red licorice.

"Brody is going to start helping me out after school," Bree said. "Technically, I think he's going to help out with watching Bailey, since my mom has been hiring me to babysit at home. That way, I can focus more of my energy on Veronica so my mom doesn't make me return him. I'm excited, but also nervous that he's going to mess up and my mom will figure out the plan, but also so tired I almost don't care. I hope it goes well."

"It'll be fine," said Malia. "And if it's not fine, you can trade with Brody, and you can watch Bailey and he can watch Veronica."

At the sound of his name, Veronica hopped down from Bree's dresser and joined the girls on the floor.

"That's actually not a bad idea, considering how well they got along at the interview," said Dot.

"You guys, Veronica is my baby. I can't leave my baby with some random person. It's my job to take care of him. What kind of parent would I be if I just left him with a random dude so I could go enjoy myself?"

"I think the thing you just described is babysitting," said Malia.

"Oh," said Bree.

"So, Malia, how is your internship going?" Dot asked.

"It is the worst thing I have ever done," Malia said.

This surprised even her. She knew that it was stressful, time-consuming, and somewhat bad for her dignity. She knew

Chelsea had only brought her on to take on the terrible grunt work. But until that moment, she hadn't realized just how horrible it was making her feel.

"That bad?" Dot said.

"Worse than you can imagine. It's, like, every time I go there, I have no idea what's going to be thrown at me and each task is worse than the last. Then, even if I do a good job, nobody says thank you. They just tell me the next thing to do. And no matter how hard I try, I cannot make this person happy."

"She sounds nuts," said Bree.

"You have no idea. Imagine Chelsea, in fifty years. But crazier."

"Could you quit?" asked Dot.

"No. I was badgered into it; there's no way my mom would let me. Plus, now it's an issue of pride. I have to show Chelsea that I can be as good as her."

"But this is about your well-being," said Bree.

"Yeah, who cares about Chelsea?" Dot chimed in. "It's impossible to win with her, anyway. If you were learning things, or enjoying yourself, I'd say to stick with it, but this is just stressing you out. And you're not even getting paid! You're turning down babysitting jobs to be miserable."

Malia sighed. Maybe her friends were right. She wanted her

old life back, when she could focus on babysitting, on running the club, on doing the things she liked—namely, watching Connor and thinking about Connor and making enough money so she could go to a concert and dance in his vicinity. It might be smarter—not to mention healthier—for her to go back to how things were before.

Malia waited until well after dinner, when all was calm in the Twiggs household. Experience had taught her this was usually the best time to ask for things—a new phone, for example, or permission to quit one's terrible unpaid internship.

"Mom?"

Malia found her mom sitting in her favorite green armchair, reading a book about cleanses. Her mom loved cleanses, which Malia found weird, since she tried to get out of cleaning things as much as possible. Sometimes her mom was into juice cleanses, which were apparently good for your body, and sometimes she was into clutter cleanses, where you threw away a bunch of stuff in order to clean your house. Her current obsession was the most confusing of all: a mental cleanse, where you got rid of negative thinking.

"Yes?" Her mom looked up from her book.

"I wanted to talk to you about something."

"Mm-hmm?" She peered at Malia through her reading glasses, which had thick red frames. Malia wasn't sure how the glasses had managed to survive through so many clutter cleanses.

"My internship . . ." She paused for a second, hoping her mom would read her mind. She didn't, so Malia continued. "Well, the thing is . . . it's terrible."

"What do you mean, terrible?"

"Oh, Mom. Ramona is, like, the witch from a storybook."

"That's not a very nice thing to say," said her mom, though she cracked the tiniest smile.

"But it's true! She yells for no reason and asks for the craziest things. I spend most of my time moving things or fixing things or making her coffee. Sometimes, she yells stuff like 'Uh-oh!' and I have to figure out what's wrong, and also fix it, with no other directions about what the problem is. And Chelsea is not helpful at all. She didn't even train me or explain how anything works. I thought I was going to be learning about business, but I'm not learning anything."

Her mom looked dismayed. Malia hoped it was a sign her mom also thought she should quit. Malia needed a life cleanse, and this was the first step.

"Malia. You may not realize it, but you are learning things.

Valuable things. You're learning how to take on assignments, and multitask, and deal with personalities that are different and perhaps a bit more challenging than the people you encounter elsewhere in your life."

Malia could already see this conversation wasn't going to go in her favor.

"Honey, if I thought this job was truly a bad fit, or that you were being mistreated in some way, of course I wouldn't allow that. But I don't want to encourage you to be a quitter."

"But it makes me want to throw things!"

"That sounds like a feeling you need to explore. Dealing with frustration is a very big part of life. Imagine if you could tackle difficult situations and not feel that way!"

Malia wondered what it must be like to have a mom who was not a career counselor. Dot's mom, for example, would probably deal with this situation by casting some sort of spell. Malia's mom, on the other hand, had a self-help book for every occasion.

"But, Mom . . ." Malia started to speak but trailed off. This conversation was pointless. Her mom would never see it from her point of view.

"Sometimes, when we're in a stressful spot, it can seem like the feeling will last forever. But this internship is temporary, as is this feeling." Her mom gave her an encouraging look. "Just try to do your best, that's all I want you to do."

Malia *was* doing her best, she thought. Her best work was being the CEO of Best Babysitters. She was good at that, and she even managed to juggle it with schoolwork. How much was one person supposed to take on in order to be doing her "best"?

Interning for Ramona was something that no one—not a sane person, not even a superhero—would be able to do well. And somehow, Malia was surviving. She should have been proud. But instead, she just felt trapped.

CHAPTER SIXTEEN

Bree

Bree hated the doctor's office. She also hated the dentist. She *especially* hated the vet, which had the same kind of icky stressful feeling as the regular doctor's office, with the added feature of making animals sad. So Bree was surprised by the scene that greeted her at the office of Veronica's new therapist, Dr. Marcy Puffin, animal behaviorist. So far, Dr. Puffin had proven wise and insightful in their initial phone consultation. But Bree was particularly excited for this first session, because her friends were coming, too.

"I can't *wait* to see what this is about," Dot said as they entered the tiny office.

"Meow," Veronica contributed.

The waiting room didn't feel like any doctor's office the

girls had ever seen. A bunch of Moroccan area rugs were strewn haphazardly in the center of the space. A wind chime dangled overhead, tinkling away. In one corner, a small artificial waterfall flowed into a koi pond, filled with brightly colored, speckled fish. Across one wall, a bookshelf was crowded with volumes with names like *Triumph of the Tiger* and *Tears for Fears—for Felines*.

"Why do I feel like my mom probably knows this person?" Dot asked, eyeing a large crystal geode, sparkling on a shelf.

"Isn't it amazing?" Bree asked.

"It's something," Malia agreed.

"I want to be just like Dr. Puffin," Bree said, then added, "I mean, when I grow up."

"Veronica," said Dr. Puffin, opening the door to her office. "Come on in."

Dr. Puffin was a youngish woman, meaning she was definitely younger than everyone's parents, but beyond that Bree had no idea how old she actually was.

"Who have we here?" she asked.

"These are my friends Dot and Malia," Bree said, "and this, of course, is Veronica." She opened the door to the cat carrier, giving Veronica free rein.

All of the girls braced themselves for impact, but much as he had with Brody, Veronica remained calm. He curled adorably in Dr. Puffin's lap, blinking his enormous eyes.

So far, visiting Dr. Puffin felt more like going to hang out with a really nice aunt who also happened to be an expert on cats.

"Veronica seems to have a lovely disposition," said Dr. Puffin, petting Veronica's wrinkly body.

"He's certainly being less violent right now," Bree said, nodding her head. "But at home, he hardly ever stands still for more than ten seconds. He destroys anything he can get his claws on. And he likes to mistake everything I own for a litter box." She sighed before adding, "I swear he does it on purpose."

"Let's play a little game, shall we?" Dr. Puffin said, speaking directly to Veronica. She held up an oversize deck of cards. "I'm going to go through a little exercise to get to know Veronica a bit better."

She held up the first card, with a picture of a fluffy white cat on it.

Veronica blinked once.

"Hm! Very interesting," said Dr. Puffin.

Next, she held up another card, with a picture of a clown on it.

"Meow," said Veronica with his usual level of emotional detachment.

"I see!" said Dr. Puffin.

She held up a third card, with a picture of a pizza on it.

Veronica started to lick his left front foot.

"Well, isn't that fascinating!" Dr. Puffin said. She put the deck of cards facedown on the low glass coffee table.

Bree had never been more confused.

"Well, maybe we should begin our session by talking about boundaries," Dr. Puffin said. At the mention of the word, Veronica climbed out of Dr. Puffin's lap and started to ascend the bookcase.

"Boundaries?" Bree said. "Like borders?"

"Yes, you might say that. Boundaries are a bit like the fixed limits between cities or countries, or even on a sports field," Dr. Puffin explained. "But what makes boundaries different is that they are often invisible. Boundaries are like borders we create for our emotions."

Bree felt lost. This seemed more like a weird geography lesson and less like a conversation about cats. Who knew parenthood was going to be so complicated?

Dr. Puffin continued. "Let's say you meet a new person and, for whatever reason, they are very angry. They have a lot of pent-up emotions and a tendency to unleash them upon the world. Would you let this person come into your home and yell at you constantly?"

"No!" said Bree. "That sounds terrible."

"That sounds like my internship," Malia said to no one in particular.

"MEOW!" Veronica yelled from the top of the bookshelf, whether in fury or agreement no one could be sure.

"Hopefully, you would try to establish healthy boundaries," said Dr. Puffin. "For example, you might limit your exposure to that person. You might speak up if they say or do something that makes you uncomfortable. And after an interaction with them, you might make time for an activity that makes you feel good, to help you heal from any emotional trauma."

"Why do I feel like I'm being lectured by my mom right now?" Dot stage-whispered to Malia.

"Now, Veronica is coming from a place where he has never lived within established boundaries," said Dr. Puffin as Veronica began to swing dramatically from the overhead light fixture. "So it is up to you, Bree, to establish them."

"I just don't understand what I'm doing wrong!" wailed Bree. She shook her fists in the air, causing her armfuls of sparkly bangle bracelets to jingle-jangle.

Veronica took this outcry as his cue to go berserk. He let out a high-pitched mewl, jumping off the light fixture and landing on the smooth glass coffee table. He arched his back like a scary cat on a Halloween decoration. Then he leaped high into the air, landing back on the top of Dr. Puffin's bookshelf, next to a potted fern. "Meow," he concluded defiantly.

The girls looked to Dr. Puffin, expecting a larger reaction from her. But she just looked at the cat with deep concentration, saying, "Hmmmmm."

"So aside from the whole boundaries thing, do you know why he is, uh, the way he is?" Malia asked.

"Pets sometimes feel scared or sad or anxious, just like people," Dr. Puffin explained. "Veronica has some learned behaviors from his past, but just like us, he creates new habits all the time."

"Meow!" said Veronica. This time it definitely sounded like agreement.

"Animals absorb a lot of energy from their environment, and Veronica is greatly affected by his time with Bree."

Veronica scowled.

Dr. Puffin continued. "That's why, in each of our sessions, the goal will be to work with both the pet *and* the owner. It's imperative that I gain a good understanding of them both."

"So you're also kind of Bree's therapist," Dot said.

"In a way, yes," said Dr. Puffin.

"Do I have to react to the flash cards, too?" Bree asked.

"No, your role is more like a detective. Our main focus is to determine what exactly sets Veronica off. He doesn't seem particularly sensitive to sound, though he does demonstrate a preference for a bit of personal space and a calm demeanor."

"I have no idea what sets him off!" Bree said, then added sadly, "Except that he doesn't like me."

"So, let's bring the focus over to you for a minute. What's going on in your life this week, Bree?" Dr. Puffin asked.

Bree brightened a little at the chance to talk about herself. That was something she didn't get to do very often. She loved her family, but they almost never gave her the chance to talk about what was going on in her life—about school, about her friends, about anything. At Bree's house, there was always someone who was talking a little louder or crying a little harder or otherwise demanding attention.

"This week has been a little challenging," Bree started. "Veronica is, well, Veronica, and I haven't been getting much sleep."

"There have been other changes, too. We hired satellite sitters for our babysitting organization," Malia cut in.

"Three new employees who could take on some of our workload," Dot added.

"They all just went through training—" Bree started to explain as Malia cut her off again.

"We thought it would help take some of the pressure off so we could focus on our other responsibilities. But it turns out being a boss actually isn't that easy," Malia said.

"Yes, and—" Bree started again, but Malia spoke over her again.

"Like, the other day one of the new hires texted me about one million times to ask me questions, and I was afraid she was messing everything up, so I ran there to check on her and then almost got fired from my internship."

"I see," said Dr. Puffin, nodding her head. "And how do *you* feel about these changes, Bree?"

Bree's heart pounded in her chest. Finally, she had the floor, but for a reason she couldn't quite figure out, she felt nervous to speak. She was overwhelmed—about Veronica, about her siblings, by confusion, by exhaustion.

"I'm not really sure how I'm feeling," she said in a small voice.

"That's okay," said Dr. Puffin in the most understanding voice Bree had ever heard an adult use. "How about this week you take some time to do something you like. An activity that is just for you. It might help you figure out how you're feeling if you have some space from all this other stuff."

"Meow," said Veronica. Without Bree realizing it, Veronica had made his way down from his bookshelf perch and started to paw gently at her leg, like a nice cat would. It was such a kind gesture, it almost made her want to cry. Veronica jumped into her lap, doing a convincing impression of a sane animal. Bree hugged him. This was how she had always pictured pet ownership. Dr. Puffin was a miracle worker!

"This reminds me: it's important that we talk about how to handle him," Dr. Puffin said. "Cats need their space, particularly Veronica. It's probably best not to hug him so securely around the neck."

"Yeah, he doesn't like being squeezed or rocked from side to side," Bree added. "He doesn't like to dance. And he definitely finds clothes to be very aggravating."

"That sounds about right." Dr. Puffin nodded. "Holding on tightly isn't the answer." She paused for a minute to let her words sink in. "Sometimes, the same advice we give about the animals can be just as useful, if not more useful, for their humans. When you squeeze Veronica too tightly, it actually causes stress for both of you, just in different ways."

"So, how does that help us?" Malia asked. She paused before adding, "You know, as people who do things not involving cats?"

"What I'm hearing is that you girls feel stressed over a situation you're trying to control but can't. The larger realization here is that no matter what, we can only ever have control over so much."

Dr. Puffin was amazingly wise. Bree wished she could come live at her office and talk to her always.

"Changes are often challenging. Letting go can feel scary, but it can also be liberating. Don't worry. Just breathe. Give things some space to let them play out." Dr. Puffin smiled. "And whenever you're feeling stressed, my advice would be not to hold on so tightly."

CHAPTER SEVENTEEN

Dot

I'm teaching him about selfie angles, read the text message. It was followed up with a photo of Pigeon and an uncharacteristically joyful-looking Aloysius, posing in front of his bookshelf. Dot stared at it for longer than felt necessary, searching for something, though she didn't know what. She and Aloysius had never taken any photos together, and it felt a little strange to see him smiling with someone else.

The picture was the latest in a long line of happy dispatches Pigeon had shared from her day. Dot was surprised Aloysius would be into such documentation. He was way more interested in how mobile devices worked than in actually using them.

Dot remembered what Dr. Puffin had said, about the importance of letting go. Was this a chance to put that into practice? The last time she had worried about texting Pigeon about babysitting, her science project had blown up.

Complicated feelings aside, Aloysius seemed happy, and that is what mattered.

What was decidedly less happy was the miniature self-refrigerating hive coolant prototype. Dot had painstakingly constructed version 2.0, with a couple adjustments to prevent overheating. Nothing was out of place. It looked absolutely perfect. According to her calculations, it should have worked beautifully. And yet, when she tried to turn it on, nothing happened.

She had already made her invention work once, sort of. So why couldn't she do it again?

"What is your problem?" Dot asked aloud, jabbing the contraption with her index finger.

"Did you say something, sweetie?" Dot's mom poked her head in the bedroom door. Their bungalow was so small it often felt impossible to have any privacy.

"No, I was just talking to myself," said Dot.

"Is everything okay?" Her mom squinted. "I'm sensing something is off with your solar plexus."

"My solar plexus is fine," said Dot. "I'm just having some issues getting this thing to work."

"It sounds like you need to meditate," said her mother, entering the room.

Dot made the conscious decision not to respond.

"What is it you're working on again?"

"A thing for bees," said Dot.

Her mom only meant well, but Dot had been very vague about her project for a number of reasons. The first was that, when it came to really important projects, Dot could be a little superstitious. She didn't believe in talking about them until they were in a stable place.

The second reason was more practical. Dot's mom was against any kind of air-conditioning, anywhere, ever. Throughout her whole life, no matter how hot it got, her mother's solution to heat waves was to wear loose cotton clothing, turn on the ceiling fan, and "pay homage to the sun." She loved to talk endlessly about how much she opposed anything that disrupted the cycles of nature. Even though Dot's project was technically good for the environment, she had a feeling her mom would still have an issue with it.

"Bees have a really special role in the natural order," said Dot's mom, taking a look around the room. Dot knew she was snooping, one of her mom's favorite activities. Luckily, all of

Dot's secret, contraband items — snacks full of preservatives, deodorant laden with chemicals — were safely hidden away.

"All right, well, I'll let you get back to it," said her mother, floating out of the room. A waft of patchouli lingered in the air.

Dot inhaled. Getting frustrated wasn't going to help anything. She needed to breathe, stay positive, and keep trying.

"Please work," she pleaded, making one tiny adjustment to the compressor.

And then, as if by magic, the prototype kicked into gear. Icy cold air blasted out of the machine. It buzzed beautifully, just like an air conditioner. Or a bee.

Dot stood back to admire her handiwork. It really was something.

She did a little celebratory dance, shaking her butt in a manner that was similar to the "waggle dance," a figure-eight movement made by honeybees to give other bees directions to nearby pollen sources. Bees were super smart, and so was Dot. She was going to win the science fair! She was going to save the world!

Dot stopped dancing to behold the tiny AC, merrily cooling away. She shivered. It was working! It was working really well. Perhaps a little too well, actually.

"Is it just me, or is it freezing in here?" called Dot's mom from the other side of the bungalow.

"Is it?" Dot said, playing dumb.

"Brrr!" Her mom appeared in the doorway, her entire body wrapped in a paisley print pashmina. She glanced around Dot's bedroom, narrowing her eyes when she spotted the hive coolant device. "What on earth is going on in here? Did you make that? Is that an *air conditioner?*"

"Not exactly."

"I thought you were doing something with bees! You know I don't believe in futzing with the natural order of things!" Her mom looked profoundly dismayed. "Why are you giving your carbon footprint an even bigger shoe size?"

"Mom! I am doing the opposite of that."

"Well, that certainly seems like an air conditioner to me!" Her mom crossed her arms, hugging the pashmina more tightly around her body.

"It is, sort of. Technically, it's a cooling device for beehives. To help combat global warming." Her mom still looked apprehensive, so Dot continued. "Ideally, the design will be updated so it could run on solar power. This experiment could very possibly save the world."

"Okay," said her mother reluctantly. "I don't entirely follow, but your heart seems to be in the right place, so I'm proud of you."

Dot smiled. She had won over the most difficult audience member, at least when it came to matters of technology. Still, she knew her mom would have her back no matter what.

Version 2.0 of the coolant device kept right on running, with no sign of stopping. It was perfect. Still, Dot couldn't rest on her laurels. This was only step one. Now she would have to make it work in an actual hive.

CHAPTER EIGHTEEN

MALIA

Malia sniffed the air. It smelled like heavy perfume, which meant that Ramona couldn't be far behind. Moments later, just as predicted, she appeared in the doorway.

"I need someone to run an errand."

Whenever Ramona requested a task from "someone," it meant that it was horrible—too horrible to assign directly to any one person—and would ultimately fall upon Malia. That's how Malia wound up "researching" the best homemade tortellini recipe in the world and organizing Ramona's extensive shoe collection by color.

"I need someone to procure crickets, dipped in chocolate." Ramona paused, and then offered by way of explanation, "It's a gift."

"Crickets?" Malia repeated.

"Yes. Crickets. They're very high in protein."

"Covered in chocolate?" Malia still wasn't sure she had heard this correctly.

"Yes. The higher the cacao content, the better, but I suppose any kind of chocolate-covered crickets will do."

Malia stood there willing her mouth to make words, but it would not.

"Thank you!" said Ramona, and flounced away.

"Your job," Chelsea said before Malia had a chance to speak.

"Where on earth am I supposed to find these?"

Chelsea sighed. "Malia, how many times do I have to tell you? Finding things is also your job."

Malia let out a sigh and began typing. Predictably, her first course of action was to scour the Internet. She typed "chocolate-covered crickets" into the search bar, and — horror of horrors — a whole screen full of results came up. Yet nothing was an exact match. Malia scanned through listings for sriracha crickets, sour-cream-and-onion crickets, cocoa-dusted scorpions, chocolate-covered bugs, and cricket protein bars. She could find zero listings for chocolate-covered crickets.

"AUUUUGGGGGH!" She let her exasperation be known.

Malia grabbed her backpack and stood up to leave.

"Where are you going?" Chelsea asked.

"To find the crickets. Obvi," spat Malia, marching out of the office. She wasn't sure how she was going to do it, but she was going to make this nonsense happen. She was a CEO after all. Her job was to make stuff work, even when she had no idea how.

The weather outside was lovely. *I could be anywhere,* thought Malia. *I could be at the park. I could be on the beach. I could be casually walking about Connor Kelly's block. I could be not-so-casually taking on just a couple more jobs to earn the money to dance with Connor at the concert. Instead, I am searching for chocolate-covered insects that jump.* At least she would get to spend some time outside while she figured out how to pull this off.

Her first stop was Monty's, the local chocolate shop. It was a small family-run business where every single item—from chocolates to lollipops to gummies of all kinds—was made by hand. The prices were pretty high, but Malia's mom would sometimes stop in for a box of mixed chocolates to put out on the table for holidays.

A jolly older woman stood behind the counter. Malia recognized her as one of the owners. Her name, Minniver, was embroidered across the pocket of her shirt.

"Good afternoon!" chimed Minniver.

Malia could only hope it was going to become one.

"Do you create custom orders?" she asked.

"Why, of course, dear, that's one of our specialties."

"So, hypothetical question: if I had a friend who was interested in a specific, uh, flavor of chocolate, you could create some custom, uh, truffles for her?"

"Righty-o," said Minniver.

"Great! Great news. I'll be back," said Malia.

Her next stop was the local pet shop.

Once upon a time, before Connor Kelly became the king of her heart, Malia had a crush on a boy named Ricardo. She knew only a few details about Ricardo, who spoke rarely and moved away in the third grade. But she remembered one very important fact: he had a pet iguana, and the iguana ate crickets. Ricardo brought the iguana in for show-and-tell, and explained in detail how his mom would take him to the pet store each week for a new batch of crickets.

"Hi there, I need to purchase some crickets!" she announced immediately upon entering.

"Aisle seven," called a guy in a blue apron.

Malia made her way to aisle seven. Sure enough, there were crickets. So many crickets. Hopping to and fro. Malia hadn't expected the crickets to be so . . . alive.

She shivered. They were so gross. Part of her wanted to turn back, but imagining the triumph she would feel when she handed Ramona a box of chocolate bugs kept her focused on the task at hand.

"Are these, like, food-grade crickets?" she asked as an employee wrangled a dozen of them into a container.

"Yeah," he said. "Your lizard will like them just fine."

Malia reasoned that Ramona sometimes resembled a lizard, so that sounded good enough for her.

How is this my life? she thought as she marched back to the chocolate shop, crickets in hand.

"All right! I'm ready for my custom order."

At the site of the crickets, Minniver's face dropped.

"Oh no, no, no." Minniver shook her head. "You want me to do what?"

"I need you to dip these crickets in chocolate."

"Why do you want to do that to perfectly good chocolate?"

Malia rolled her eyes and made a face that meant, *Oh, Minniver. I agree.*

"Don't ask," she said. "It wasn't my idea. But I really need you to do it. It's a very important gift."

Minniver just stared at Malia, wondering if she was for real.

"I have to touch them?"

"I can help!" said Malia. "I'm desperate."

"Fine," Minniver said. "Under one condition. You must never tell anyone I did this. I don't need us getting a reputation that we have bugs jumping around our shop."

"It's a deal," said Malia, breathing a sigh of relief.

The moment when Malia marched into Ramona Abernathy's house wielding chocolate-covered crickets would go down as quite possibly the very best moment of her entire life. Her mom was right; the bad feeling didn't last. It got replaced with a much, much better one.

"Where have you been?" asked Chelsea. "That took forever."

Malia held up the golden box from Monty's Chocolate Shop. She didn't say a word. She didn't have to.

"Oh my goodness," said Chelsea. "You did it. You actually did it!"

"Of course I did it," said Malia. She kept on walking, right into Ramona's office.

Chelsea followed close behind.

"Ramona, I have your chocolate-covered crickets," Malia said. "There are a dozen of them. Made fresh, especially for you."

"We hope you like them," said Chelsea.

"Yes," said Malia. "*I* really hope you like them." She smiled directly at Chelsea as she added, "I tried my best. After all, finding things is *my* job. And I take great pride in it."

Ramona smiled so widely even her eyes lit up. It reminded Malia of a department store Santa. Until this moment, she hadn't known Ramona was capable of looking so jolly, yet Malia had just made it happen.

Meanwhile, Chelsea gave her a look of death. It was the same look Malia had seen a million times before — in the hallway before bed, in the rearview mirror, over the dinner table at pizza night. But this time, for the very first time, it was happening because Malia had won. It felt amazing. And for that, she would have fetched all the crickets in the universe.

CHAPTER NINETEEN

Bree

For the first time in a long time, Bree felt hopeful. Today, Brody would be taking on his first babysitting job: helping out with Bailey after school. With Brody lending a hand, Bree would be able to offer Veronica her undivided attention and actually implement some of Dr. Puffin's suggestions.

Brody arrived just after three, carrying his skateboard in hand.

"Sick house," said Brody, stopping just inside the front door. "It feels, like, so modern in here."

Bree wasn't exactly sure what that meant, so she just said, "Thank you."

Bailey came bounding into the vestibule, eating a tortilla chip.

"Brody, this is my brother, Bailey," she said. "Bailey, this is my friend Brody. He's my age and goes to Fratford Academy. Like I said, he's a babysitter-in-training, and so he's going to hang out with both of us after school sometimes."

"Hey, bro," said Brody, giving a little wave.

"Whoa! You have the KZ-7s!" said Bailey, pointing to Brody's sneakers. "Those are crazy hard to find."

Brody's face brightened. "Are you into skating?" he asked.

"Yeah!" said Bailey.

"Me too!" said Brody.

"Wanna see my stuff?" Bailey asked, excited.

"Of course," said Brody.

Bailey took off running to his room, with Brody right behind.

Bree let out a satisfied sigh. They would get along just fine.

Bree hurried up the stairs behind them but continued past her brother's bedroom. She heard the boys excitedly chattering inside and reasoned she might as well take this moment to check on the cat. "I'll catch up with you guys in a minute!" she called, scurrying into her own room and closing the door behind her.

"Veronica! What have you been—" She hadn't even finished her sentence when she saw exactly what Veronica was up to. He had once again become "confused" about the location of the litter box. This time, he had left something inside her makeup organizer.

Veronica watched as Bree cleaned up the offending "present."

"Meow," said Veronica, sweetly perched atop the comforter, as though assuming a pleasant demeanor would somehow distract from the larger situation.

"Veronica, this is NOT your litter box!" Bree grumbled.

"Meow?" Veronica offered.

Bree was so angry she picked up a glittery cloud-shaped pillow and launched it across the room. It hit the back of the closed bedroom door, landing on the ground with a thud.

Veronica watched the pillow fly through the air, growing visibly perturbed. And, as it had happened so many times before, he went on a rampage. He bounded from surface to surface, knocking every last item onto the ground, meowing all the way.

"Veronica," Bree said calmly, trying to mimic Dr. Puffin's tone of voice. "I need you to calm down."

Bree remembered Dr. Puffin's advice, about how an animal's emotions often mirror the emotions of their owner. She breathed deeply, in and out for counts of five, trying to keep calm, too.

What would Bree do if a child she was babysitting were having a meltdown? That was easier. She knew exactly how to talk a child down. She had successfully convinced the Woo girls not to jump on the furniture or slide down the bannister or light things on fire. Bree hadn't expected it, but at that moment, she felt a pang. She really missed babysitting. Who could have predicted that watching children could ever be (so much) more enjoyable than watching cats?

"Meow," said Veronica.

"That's better." Bree scooped Veronica into her arms. "See how much I love you?"

Bree hugged the wriggly kitty. Maybe if she hugged him enough, he would understand how much she cared for him. Suddenly remembering Dr. Puffin's advice, Bree relaxed her grip. She wanted to hug Veronica but didn't want to squeeze him too hard. Veronica relaxed a bit in her arms. Was it possible she was getting through to him? Could he feel her love?

"GAK! GAK! GAK!" And with that, Veronica vomited all over her sparkly hoodie.

Bree stood in the center of her room, stunned and covered in cat puke.

"Meow," said Veronica calmly, as he leaped from her arms and padded across the floor.

Bree unzipped her hoodie and deposited it into her hamper, where it joined a very large assortment of clothing that Veronica had soiled in some way over the course of the past few days. She would have to wear her plain T-shirt for the rest of the evening.

"Veronica." Bree inhaled sharply. "I think we could both use some more space. Let's see what Bailey and Brody are up to, okay?"

Veronica blinked slowly.

Bree opened her bedroom door, and Veronica bounded out. Bree trudged down the stairs after him. Maybe spending some time around people would be a nice change. She heard shouts and laughter coming from downstairs. It sounded so joyful. Bree missed joy.

Bree followed the *glink, glink* sounds of golden coins being collected in a video game. Sure enough, Brody and Bailey were on the family room couch, racing each other around a virtual track.

"Heeeeeeeeey," said Brody, never taking his eyes from the screen.

Veronica hopped on the couch next to Brody and curled up into a little ball. Bree couldn't believe her eyes. Veronica was acting, well, like a cat.

Veronica blinked sweetly in Bree's direction, like he wanted to rub it in.

Bree sat on the floor, unsure of what to do. Brody's presence had somehow managed to calm both Bailey and Veronica into sitting still. Bree was suddenly left with nobody to babysit.

Bree stretched out on the soft carpet, watching the scene before her. She breathed the deepest breath she had taken in a long time. She closed her eyes. Just for a second, because it felt so nice. Maybe just one more second, she thought. It felt so wonderful to rest.

The *glink, glink* of the golden coins lulled her into a deep sleep.

"TACO!" yelled Olivia, followed by a crash.

Bree immediately opened her eyes. She wasn't sure how much time had passed, but she was in the family room, alone. What had happened to Brody and Bailey? WHAT HAD HAPPENED TO VERONICA?

Bree scrambled to her feet and followed the sounds of commotion coming from the kitchen.

Nearly all of Bree's family—her mom, Marc, Bailey,

Emma, and Olivia—had just arrived home and gathered in the kitchen.

Emma and Olivia were just taking their backpacks off and buzzing from their evening dance class, while Bree's mom was taking various items out of the fridge. Marc was in the process of setting the table, where Brody and Bailey politely sat.

"I can name the presidents in order!" shouted Emma.

"TACO!" exclaimed Olivia. "TACO! TACO!"

"Well, not all the presidents, but most of the presidents," Emma corrected herself. "Wanna hear?"

"I'd love to hear!" said Brody, which was sweet, since normally everyone was too focused on Olivia to pay much attention to Emma's displays of knowledge.

"George Washington! John Adams! Thomas Jefferson! James Madison!" Emma started.

Bree approached the table.

"Oh, heeey!" Brody said, waving.

"Um, everyone, this is my friend Brody," Bree said, by way of introduction.

"We gathered that!" Marc laughed.

"Hi, sweetie," said her mom as soon as she caught sight of Bree. "It seems like you've had a very successful evening."

"Meow," said Veronica. He was curled up in Chocolate Pudding's acorn-shaped cat bed, still pretending to be sane.

Bree didn't have the heart to tell her mom she'd accidentally taken a nap, so she just nodded.

"James Monroe! John Quincy Adams! Andrew Jackson!" Emma continued.

"Veronica seems so content," observed Bree's mom. "And there don't appear to be any surprises in any of the planters, or in the piano, for that matter."

"Can Brody stay for taco night?" asked Bailey.

"I don't see why not, as long as it's okay with Brody's family," said Marc, who was now grilling fish on the stovetop.

"I'd love to," said Brody.

Bree immediately thought of the last taco night, and how it had ended in disaster, with Veronica yakking in the piano. Now, with Brody here, taco night could go as planned—with everyone eating tacos. What's more, the entire family appeared to be having a wonderful time. Brody was already fitting in like he was a long-lost sibling—which, to be clear, Bree did not want any more of, because her family already had enough members. But he was a very good hire. This was, she reasoned, the best possible scenario.

Bree pulled out a chair and sat down next to Brody.

"Martin Van Buren! Um . . . Um . . ." Emma scrunched up her face in thought.

"Did you, like, drug Veronica?" Bree whispered.

Brody looked at her with horror.

"I know this! Hold on, lemme think of it!" Emma said.

"Of course not," Brody whispered back. "Why would you say that?"

"He's just so . . ." Bree peered under the table, where Veronica was slowly licking his back paw. "I've never seen him this chill."

"Maybe it's my vibe," Brody said with a shrug.

Marc placed the grilled fish on the table, alongside the tortillas and toppings.

"Taco night is served!" he said with a flourish. "Dig in!"

Bree watched as Brody served himself a taco and took a big bite. From her seat several inches away, Bree stared at his face as he chewed. She had never noticed it before, but Brody was actually kind of cute. Handsome, even. It was weird.

He looked over at her. "What?" he asked. "Do I have something on my face?"

"No. I mean, I wasn't looking at you," Bree lied, and went back to adding more cabbage to her taco.

She had been nervous about how today would go, but

clearly there was nothing to fear. Bailey loved Brody, heck even Veronica loved him, and now the whole family loved him, too. Brody was so funny and charming that it felt like he had been here all along.

Bree wondered how different the world must be for a boy. Sometimes it seemed like all they had to do was show up and say a few nice things, and maybe occasionally smile, and people would give them whatever they wanted.

"These tacos are great," Brody said, flashing a giant smile.

"I'm so glad you like them!" Bree's mom beamed.

"Taco! Taco!" Olivia chanted.

"They're a family tradition," Marc added.

"WILLIAM HENRY HARRISON!" Emma practically exploded.

"I'll be back in a sec!" Bree said, pulling her chair out and slipping out of the room.

Bree needed to sneak away for a minute, as she sometimes did during family commotions. She loved being around the whole group, but right now, she wanted to check her phone and text her friends and see what she'd missed in the time since she'd fallen asleep.

Bree started up the stairs, when she heard a tiny voice behind her.

"Meow."

Bree was surprised to discover Veronica scaling the steps behind her.

He followed her all the way back up to her bedroom. It was so uncharacteristic of him—was it possible he was actually seeking out her company? Was he finally ready to be friends?

The evening had been a success so far, but Bree didn't want to push her luck. Who knows how long it would be before he decided to have a meltdown on top of something expensive?

Veronica immediately hid under the bed. Only his eyes were visible, glowing in the shadows. Bree tried not to be insulted by this.

"Veronica! I think this is going to work out!"

"Meow?" Veronica stared at her, unblinking.

"With Brody helping out with Bailey, I can focus all my extra time on you!"

Veronica did not react to this.

"We can work through the suggestions from Dr. Puffin. And eventually, maybe you can act normal all the time! Maybe one day, I can even hug you."

Veronica continued staring.

"It's fine, Veronica, I know you're a cat and you aren't big on expressions. You can play it cool as much as you want. But I know you're excited."

"Meow," said Veronica. His tone didn't really give much away, one way or another.

CHAPTER TWENTY

MALIA

Malia sat at the lunch table, all alone.

She had called a lunch meeting of Best Babysitters, because she needed to collect funds from the new hires, and also because if there was one thing she had learned from her time with Ramona, it was that important people liked to take lunch meetings. But so far, none of the other members of this meeting were taking punctuality very seriously.

Malia bit into her cafeteria mozzarella stick. It didn't behave the way a mozzarella stick should—it didn't form one long, delicious string of cheese, the way the mozzarella sticks at Marvelous Ray's Arcade did. It wasn't even particularly chewy, like the frozen boxed mozzarella sticks she sometimes ate at home. Instead, it almost snapped in half, which was troubling.

Malia chewed pensively as she watched Bree approaching the table.

"Did you buy lunch today? That's brave," said Bree, taking her lunch bag out of her backpack.

"I did, but I'm starting to regret it. How did things go with Brody last night?" asked Malia.

"Great!" said Bree. "Everyone absolutely loves him, especially Veronica."

"That's great! So the cat managed to behave himself?"

"Yes!" said Bree. She grew thoughtful for a moment. "Although, this morning, Veronica did manage to poop in the middle of the kitchen table."

"Veronica did WHAT?" said Pigeon, placing her perfect-looking black leather purse on the table and taking a seat.

"Pooped. On the table," said Bree.

"We're talking about a cat named Veronica, not Veronica the pop star," Malia clarified.

"Oh," said Pigeon. There was a pause for a moment. "Still, that's pretty gross."

Just then, Dot arrived. She stood, eyeing the table for longer than was comfortable. Finally, she took a seat on the far side of the table, a good distance away from the other girls, including Pigeon.

"How's the science fair project going?" asked Pigeon.

"Great," said Dot with false cheer. "How's yours going?"

"Oh, it couldn't be better," said Pigeon.

Bree looked back and forth between them like she was watching a tennis match.

"So! Time to get this meeting underway," said Malia. "I am pleased to announce that we are closing in on our ultimate goal of concert tickets."

"For the Veronica concert?" Pigeon said, wrinkling her nose up like she had just tasted something awful. "THAT'S your goal?"

"It's not my goal," said Dot.

"It's a goal," said Malia. "Any business guru worth their salt will tell you it's good to have specific, measurable goals. ANYWAY—"

"Wait, where's Sage?" Dot interrupted.

Across the cafeteria, Sage was still chatting with the boys at her table, waving her hands and laughing. Malia wished she knew what they were talking about.

"SAAAGE!" Malia called, cupping her hands around her mouth like a dad in a yard that was trying to get a golden retriever to come inside before a rainstorm.

Sage looked up and made a gesture that meant, "Yeah, sure, in a minute."

"SAAAGE!" Malia called again. Sometimes the golden

retriever didn't want to come inside, Malia thought, but that didn't stop the dad from calling until it did.

This time, Sage stood up and came over to the table.

"Hey, Malia," she said.

"How did everything go at the Gregory house?" Malia asked.

She knew she was supposed to let go a little, but once a CEO, always a CEO.

"Oh, it was fun. We played soccer in the yard and the kids had Popsicles."

Soccer in the *yard?* The same yard with the glorious view of Connor Kelly's house? Malia was instantly jealous. Her soul wanted to cry. "That's great!" she said instead.

"Yeah, I'm really enjoying sitting for them. They're so adorable," Sage said. "Oh! I almost forgot. I have to run, but here's the split of the wages from last night." Sage dug around in her backpack and deposited a stack of bills in Malia's hand. Pigeon opened up her beautiful purse and did the same.

"I'll see you guys later!" Sage called. Malia watched as she made her way back to the table full of boys. Clearly, she didn't have any pressing things to attend to, unless you counted flirting.

"Great meeting. I should really be going," said Pigeon, excusing herself from the table.

"Lovely chatting with you!" Dot called after her sweetly.

Malia gave the money a very quick count, to confirm what she already knew: it was exactly the amount they still needed to secure the Veronica concert tickets. She had expected it to go down exactly this way, but there was something so liberating about having the money in hand.

It was happening! Everything was happening.

"Guess what?" Malia said, first confirming Pigeon was out of earshot.

"Um . . . something about Connor Kelly?" Bree guessed.

"Good guess, but no," Malia said.

"Um . . . Ramona sent you a crazy text even though it's during the school day?" Bree tried.

"Ugh, no. Thank goodness. One more try."

Bree scrunched her face up in thought. "Um . . . I don't know. I give up."

"We have enough money to buy the Veronica tickets!"

"AHHHHHHHH!" Bree screamed so loud that not one, but three neighboring lunch tables turned to gawk at them.

"Nothing to see here, folks. Carry on," said Malia.

"Whoa!" said Dot. She seemed excited.

"I'm sorry, do I sense excitement coming from the general direction of one Dot Marino?" Malia teased.

"I'm excited for you guys," Dot said.

"Should we go to the mall to look for outfits?" Malia asked. Now that the concert was definitely a go, she had to make sure she looked her best.

"AHHHHHHHHH!" Bree screamed again.

This time, four neighboring tables turned to see what the deal was. Normally causing a scene at lunchtime was not an acceptable thing to do. But Malia was too excited to be mortified. Everything was falling into place.

CHAPTER TWENTY-ONE

Dot

At the age of thirteen, in the town of Playa del Mar, there were few things more enjoyable than the mall. With all the time she'd recently spent focused on the science fair, let alone training new club members and keeping up with schoolwork, Dot had forgotten just how joyous mall roaming could be.

"This is so nice, being here together," Bree said. "I feel like I've been let out of prison."

"You guys. Big picture . . ." Malia clapped her hands. "We are entrepreneurs, and we've successfully completed our first expansion. We've DOUBLED the size of our organization, and we are earning more money without doing more work. And now we are rewarding ourselves with the concert of our dreams. We deserve to celebrate!"

Honestly, Dot felt a little stressed. Every hour spent wandering the mall was an hour not spent observing air-conditioned bees. Plus, she didn't need to buy a new outfit for the Veronica concert, because she already knew exactly what she was going to wear—an outfit that was simple and sophisticated and slightly glamorous and just a little bit grungy, like Veronica herself. Not because Dot cared about Veronica, of course. She just liked to be prepared.

Still, she supposed that everyone deserved a break sometimes. And what better way to spend a break, she reasoned, than by eating all of the glorious foods the mall had to offer?

Her mother's organic grocery shopping had gotten even more restrictive as of late, so Dot wanted to make up for it in the grandest way. Unfortunately, she still had to be economical, since the bee coolant parts and concert tickets had eaten up nearly all of her funds. So she settled on something sweet and something savory: cinnamon-sugar pretzel nuggets and an order of nacho bites.

"Are you sure you don't want a pizza, too?" asked Malia, eyeing Dot's bounty.

"I thought we were here to celebrate the fruits of our labor," Dot said.

"But technically, those are not fruits," said Malia. "Those are pretzels."

"We should do something really, really fun!" said Bree.

"Do you want to go to MeowTown?" Malia asked Bree. A valid suggestion, since MeowTown had long been established as one of Bree's favorite places on Earth.

"NO. I do NOT want to go to MeowTown," said Bree. A look of panic flashed across her face.

"Wow. Has Veronica put you off cats?" Dot asked.

"I thought it was going better now that Brody was helping," Malia said.

"I—I—" Bree struggled to find her words. "I still love cats. I just need a break right now."

"Do we need to be worried?" Dot had never seen Bree look so traumatized before. She missed her happy-go-lucky friend—the one who wanted to secretly shop for toys and bust out in original choreography and cover the world in sparkles.

They wandered a bit more, speeding up to avoid the overzealous perfume sample lady who offered to spritz them, then chased them even after they said no. Malia was looking to and fro, craning her neck like she was searching for someone.

"Malia, what's up? Were you secretly hired to do mall surveillance?" Dot asked.

"No. Nothing's up. Why would you ask that?"

"Are you looking for Connor?" Bree asked.

"NO," Malia said, but her face said otherwise. "Okay, yes."

"Would you even talk to him if you saw him?" Dot teased.

"That is beside the point," Malia said, stealing a pretzel nugget. "But I might."

They strolled on, nary a Connor in sight. Then Bree spotted something even more troubling.

"Monsterface alert! Danger! Danger!" said Bree.

Dot almost choked on her pretzel nugget.

"Zelda Hooper," whispered Malia with a fear and disgust usually reserved for words like "cockroach" or "dragon."

Dot looked up to see Zelda, meanest of the mean girls, coming out of Phoebe's, the trendiest and most expensive boutique. Her face was scrunched up like she was very, very angry at something, although Dot knew from experience that it always looked that way. Ever since kindergarten, Zelda had been a mean girl. She was so mean, it was a pretty safe assumption she had just been born that way.

Today she was wearing a leather jacket over ripped-up jeans

and combat boots. Even her clothes looked mean. Her long red hair, though, looked very, very pretty.

"What do we do?" Bree said.

"Run the other way, obvi," said Malia.

The girls made an abrupt about-face and started speed-walking in the opposite direction.

Zelda had a long history of bullying. Every school year, she liked to choose a different target and then try to make their lives miserable. In second grade, her target had been Malia. In third grade, it was Dot. In fifth grade, it was Bree. Her tactics involved rumors, mean notes, evil pranks—all of it "anonymous," but all of it obviously Zelda.

"Remember when she filled my locker with sand? And I got in trouble for making the hallway look like a beach and I couldn't prove that I wasn't the one who did it?" Bree asked.

"Why are there people like Zelda in the world?" wondered Malia.

"Variety. Or something," said Dot.

"Oh, look!" said Malia the lookout. "There's Wendy and Aloysius."

Aloysius and his mom, Wendy, were walking toward them. As usual, both of them were dressed entirely in black.

"Hi, girls!" Wendy said warmly. "What are you all up to?"

"Oh, you know, just taking a break from being responsible," said Malia.

"Where are you guys coming from?" Dot asked.

"We were at MeowTown!" said Aloysius.

Bree visibly shuddered.

"Girls, I've been meaning to tell you," Wendy started, "I am so happy with how things have been going with the new sitter! Pigeon is lovely, so gracious and smart. She and Aloysius seem to be getting along really well, too." She dropped her voice to a whisper. "And you know how he can be kind of difficult at first, so that's really saying something."

"That's so wonderful to hear!" said Malia.

It was wonderful, Dot supposed, but it also felt strange to hear. Aloysius had been her favorite client, and she thought their bond was special. Hearing how easily Pigeon replaced her made her feel hollow inside. She reminded herself that all of this was happening for a reason. The satellite sitters were allowing her to focus on the science fair. And the more time Pigeon "science is my thing" de Palma spent babysitting, the better it was for everyone.

"Enjoy the rest of your day!" Wendy said.

"Bye!" said Aloysius.

"Bye!" The girls all waved.

Still, watching Aloysius and his mom head in the other direction, Dot couldn't help but feel like a little part of herself had gone away.

CHAPTER TWENTY-TWO

MALIA

MALIA!"

Malia marveled at how different it could be when different people said your name. The same word that inspired such joy when it came out of Connor's mouth could inspire such dread when her mom used it to express disappointment. Just a few short weeks ago, she had no idea how panicked she could be upon hearing the sound of her own name. That is, until Ramona was the one to yell it.

"MALIAAAAAA!"

"I'm coming!" Malia trilled, scuttling into Ramona's office. She could only imagine what inane task she would be asked to complete, or what task she was about to discover she had already messed up.

But when she entered the room, Ramona looked pleased,

almost happy. (Or at least, as happy as her face was able to look.) She also wasn't alone. The most beautiful boy Malia had ever seen was on his way out of the office.

He was almost too glorious to look at. He was—Malia couldn't believe she was thinking such a thing—even more attractive than Connor Kelly.

"Malia, this is my grandson, Martin. He just moved to Playa del Norte, just to the north of us, and is staying with me while his parents are getting the new house settled."

Malia couldn't speak.

"Nice to meet you," said Martin's beautiful, beautiful mouth before he exited the room.

"Malia. Please have a seat." Ramona motioned to the pink upholstered chairs directly across from her desk. Malia sat, realizing she had never actually perched in one of these chairs before.

She braced herself for whatever scolding was about to come next.

"I want to let you know that I've been observing you," Ramona said.

Malia imagined a creepy surveillance camera, watching her every move.

"And I have been very happy with your performance."

This was certainly unexpected. Malia didn't know what to say.

"Thank you, Ramona."

"When Chelsea and I discussed taking on another intern, especially someone as junior as you, I must admit, I was apprehensive. But you have proven yourself to be curious, creative, driven, and inventive. Sometimes, you've managed to find the thing when even I wasn't clear about what the thing was! I think these qualities will serve you well in your own business endeavors."

Malia couldn't believe her ears! The impossible-to-please woman was singing her praises!

"When the time comes, I will be quite happy to serve as a reference for you."

"Thank you very much, Ramona."

Malia wasn't sure if Chelsea was able to hear the conversation from where she sat in the main office, but when she walked back to her desk, Chelsea's expression told her all she needed to know.

"Hello, big sister," Malia said, assuming the singsong tone Chelsea used whenever she was gloating about one of her many triumphs.

Chelsea was typing furiously, her face pink with anger.

"How's it going out here?"

Chelsea kept typing, never looking away from her screen.

"Is there anything I can help you with?" Malia asked her.

Chelsea just shook her head no.

"All right, well, if you have any questions, or if you'd like any *advice*," Malia emphasized that word, knowing how much it would bother her sister, "or any assistance from the number one employee," Malia continued, enjoying how Chelsea bristled, "you know where to find me."

Malia took a little bit of a detour on her walk home. She was feeling like a winner, and winners were entitled to a victory lap. Not only was she a winner with Ramona, but she was getting her prized concert tickets. Everything was falling into place.

Now all she had to do was figure out exactly where the other kids from school were sitting so she could try to finagle a seat near theirs. For this reason, her victory lap went right past the street of one Connor Kelly. Sadly, Connor was nowhere to be seen, but the thought of his proximity was enough to make Malia feel even happier.

And then, something happened.

"Hey, Malia!"

Malia stopped in her tracks. She knew that voice anywhere. It was the voice that haunted her dreams. It was audible sunshine. It was he.

She turned, her heart in her throat. This was it. This was the moment she'd been waiting for. Connor had called to her, seemingly on purpose. Now it was time to fulfill her destiny.

There he was, only a few feet away, wearing an adorable gray T-shirt and walking alongside . . . SAGE?

Malia's heart stopped beating. The Earth stopped spinning. Suddenly, she was floating above herself, looking down at her own body as it walked through a cruel, cruel world she had no desire to be a part of.

Okay, so that's not really what happened, but that's exactly what it felt like. Malia took a deep breath and tried to speak.

"Hey, guys," Malia finally said.

"Hi, Malia!" Sage said with a painful amount of glee. "Where are you off to?"

"Oh, you know, a party," Malia lied. She hoped it sounded true.

"Who's having a party?" Connor asked.

"My friend." Malia tried to think on her feet. "Sammy. Who goes to school in another town. Yeah. I'd totally invite you to come, but I think it's kind of a small thing."

"That's okay. We're on our way to Marvelous Ray's," said Sage.

"Yeah, Marvelous Ray's," parroted Connor.

"Oh," said Malia.

"We'd invite you to come, but you obviously already have plans, so . . ." Sage trailed off.

Malia wanted to scream. They were going to Marvelous Ray's arcade-slash-temple-of-joy? TOGETHER? Like, on a date? What was going on here?

And Malia could have gone with them, but no. She had to open her big mouth to try to sound cool, and now she would look like a fool if she backtracked.

"I had no idea you guys were"—Malia could barely get the next word out—"friends."

"It's the funniest thing," Sage said, lightly touching Connor's arm in a way that made Malia's face feel like it might melt off at any second. "I was babysitting at the Gregorys', and Connor saw me leaving. He waved me over, because he actually thought I was you!"

"Ha. So funny," Malia said, without a hint of humor.

"I saw a striped shirt and was like, must be Malia. But it wasn't you. It was her," said Connor.

"So then I asked if Connor wanted to play video games," Sage said.

"And I was like, yeah. Because, you know, I like video games," Connor said. It might have been the longest sentence he'd ever spoken directly to Malia. If only it hadn't been about Sage.

"I like video games," Malia offered helplessly. She didn't actually. But she was interested in any activity involving Connor.

"Maybe we should all play sometime," Connor said.

"YES!" Malia said, much too loudly.

"Definitely! Sometime soon," said Sage. She touched Connor's arm again. Malia's heart sank.

"Well, bye, Malia!" said Connor.

"Bye," Malia squeaked.

And with that, the two of them walked on. On to Marvelous Ray's, and the rest of their wonderful afternoon, and the rest of their wonderful lives.

Malia didn't know what to do. She didn't know what to think, she didn't know what to feel. Who did Sage think she was? She could take a cut of Malia's babysitting wages. She could even take her place in the hearts of the neighborhood children. But this! This was another level. She could never take her Connor.

Malia huffed. So maybe he had never actually been *her* Connor. But even so, Connor was like the sun. Connor was like the blueness of the sky. Connor was meant for everyone to enjoy. He belonged to no one. Certainly not Sage.

Malia fought the urge to pull a Veronica and vandalize everything in sight. She didn't know how she would pull it off, though logistics had never been a problem before. She would find a way. She would get Sage a new hobby and reclaim her Connor. She would make everything right.

CHAPTER TWENTY-THREE

Bree

Bree was so excited. She felt like the human equivalent of glitter, or maybe popcorn. Yes, popcorn! Definitely popcorn.

Today wasn't any old day; it was a birthday day! It wasn't her birthday, but it was almost the next best thing—it was Bailey's birthday. That meant cake and decorations and partying and happiness, right in her very own home. Bree hadn't been this excited since Malia told her they had enough money to see Veronica (the person, not the cat).

Brody arrived after school, as he had before, but this time he was carrying a balloon in the shape of a sneaker.

"WHOA!" said Bailey. He was really excited about this balloon. If Bree had any idea he would have appreciated a sneaker balloon so much, she would have gotten him one years ago. Or ever.

Within minutes of his arrival, Brody worked his magic on Veronica (the cat, not the person), petting his hairless body and lulling the little feline into a deep and restful slumber. With the cat safely napping inside his plush cat pod that lived in Bree's bedroom, everyone was safe to enjoy the afternoon, knowing that minimal damage was being incurred.

Bree was so ready to celebrate.

"So! Do you all want to do something special? For Bailey's birthday?" she asked.

"Skateboards!" said Bailey.

"Yeah!" said Brody.

"Oh," said Bree. "But I don't know how."

"That's okay! You can watch!" said Bailey.

Bree didn't want to watch; Bree wanted to celebrate. But she figured being present was better than nothing. That's how Bree found herself sitting on the curb, holding the sneaker balloon and watching Bailey and Brody have fun without her.

First Bailey and Brody skateboarded back and forth down the street, practicing jumping up and over the curb. Then Brody taught Bailey how to do something called a nollie, and helped him work on his form. Once Bailey mastered it, they both jumped around with excitement. Then Brody made a video of Bailey doing a nollie so he could show all his friends that it had happened.

Even though Bree had never skateboarded before, she would have loved to try. She would have loved to do anything (okay, maybe not *anything*, but certainly a bunch of things) with her brother on his birthday. But Bree was completely left out.

Bree cheered from the sidelines, but it really wasn't the same.

Finally, after many, many minutes of this, Bree's mom appeared and called them inside for cake.

The kitchen was set up a little like taco night, but instead of toppings, the counter was lined with birthday things—a cake in the shape of a skateboard, plus big plastic bowls full of party snacks. There were different kinds of potato chips and tortilla chips and popcorn and three kinds of candy.

"Can Brody stay for cake?" Bailey asked.

"Of course!" Bree's mom said, as if it had never been a question.

"This is so much fun!" Brody said, his face lighting up like a kid on a commercial for Disneyland. It was almost like he'd never seen a birthday party before.

"BIRT-DAY! BAIDY!" yelled Olivia, toddling into the room. "BWODY! YAY!"

Even Olivia was in love with Brody, Bree thought with a sigh.

"Did you know that the practice of serving birthday cake started in the Middle Ages?" asked Emma, taking a seat at the table.

"I did not know that," Brody said.

"In Germany!" Emma supplied, excited that someone was interested. "It was called Kinderfest!"

Once everyone had gathered, Bree's mom dimmed the light and lit the candles—ten candles, and one more for good luck. Bree couldn't believe Bailey was ten! She remembered when he was just a baby and she had tried to stick buttons up his nose. It didn't feel that long ago.

The family sang "Happy Birthday," then paused so Bailey could blow out the candles.

"Make a wish!" said Bree. Wish making was Bree's very favorite part of birthdays. Bree loved making wishes all the time, but there was something about a birthday wish that made it feel so destined to come true.

"So you go to Fratford?" Bree's stepdad, Marc, asked Brody, as they all dug into the cake.

"That's correct," Brody said.

"That's a fine school!" Marc said. "One of my partners' sons goes there."

Brody then proceeded to sing the Fratford Academy school song, which involved a lot of cheering and hollering. He made different voices for all the parts. It was a huge hit.

"Those voices are amazing!" said Marc, laughing so hard that tears appeared in the corners of his eyes. "Where did you learn how to do that?"

"I love to watch funny movies," Brody said with a shrug. "Lately, I've been watching Monty Python."

"I LOVE Monty Python!" said Marc.

"We should all watch a movie together tonight!" Bailey suggested.

"That's a great idea! Brody is such a hoot," said Bree's mom adoringly.

"BWODY DA BEST!" said Olivia. She was so excited that she threw a fistful of cake. It sailed across the table, where it hit Bree right between the eyes. Somehow, no one else saw this happen.

"Mom! Olivia threw cake at me!" Bree said.

Her mom didn't hear her.

"Can Brody sleep over?" Bailey said at the exact same moment. It was his birthday, so of course, everyone heard him.

"Well that's a fun idea!" said Bree's mom. "Brody, do you think it would be all right with your parents?"

"I'd love that! Let me call them and check!" he said, excusing himself for a moment.

Bree was seriously confused. The other thirteen-year-old boys she knew were overwhelmingly awkward. They didn't make jokes, and they certainly didn't want to hang out with other people's families. How had she managed to find the one boy who was capable of taking over hers?

With Brody gone, Bree decided to seize the moment and try to get her brother's full attention.

"Bailey, I can't believe you're ten!" she said. "Happy, happy birthday!"

She enveloped him in a giant hug.

"Do you know what I wished for when I blew out the candles?" Bailey whispered into her ear.

"What?" she answered.

"I wished that Brody could be our brother and live with us forever!"

Bree's heart sank. She supposed she should have been

touched that Bailey wanted to share his secret wish with her, but why did it have to be about Brody? Why did *everything* suddenly seem to be about Brody?

When she had suggested that he help out with babysitting, she had hoped everyone would like him, but she never expected they would like him this much. Bailey's wish aside, it felt like Brody was on his way to becoming a new family member. But Bree's family didn't need any new family members. They already had too many of those to begin with. Plus, Brody was the same age as Bree, so it's not like he was adding anything new. He was just making her seem less special.

"They said I can stay!" said Brody. Everyone cheered. Bree's cheer was not quite as loud as everyone else's.

"Should we open presents?" Bree's mom asked.

"Yeah!" Bailey and Brody cheered at the same time.

"Uh, I'm not feeling very well," Bree lied, pushing her chair out from the table. "I'm sorry, can you please excuse me for a minute?" She bolted out of the kitchen and back to her bedroom. She might have looked dramatic, but she knew she needed to cry, and she didn't want to cry in front of the rest of her family. Not on a birthday day, of all days.

She no longer felt like glitter. She no longer felt like

popcorn. She felt way more like the "presents" Veronica kept leaving in her makeup organizer.

Bree ran up the stairs and closed her bedroom door behind her. She stood for a moment with her back against the door, then slid down it, until she was sitting on the floor. It was there she started to cry.

"Meow."

In a very unusual display of sanity, Veronica appeared from under the bed and came to take a seat next to her. He was sitting still. And in an even more unusual display of understanding, he did not move when Bree began to pet him.

"Veronica, I feel like you're the only one who is on my side," said Bree, petting his wrinkly, hairless body. "And you don't really like me, do you?"

Veronica might have been crazy, but he wasn't dumb.

He knew it was best not to answer.

CHAPTER TWENTY-FOUR

Dot

At last, it was judgment day. Literally. The Playa del Mar middle school gymnasium was filled with tables, each one topped with a hopeful student's science project. Dot stood in front of her entry—the hive coolant device attached to a hive, all of it surrounded by a mesh cage, to ensure there would be no accidental stinging. It had all come together at the last minute, not to mention been a real challenge to transport from her home to the school. The apparatus barely fit into the back of her mom's Prius. But everything had worked out in the end.

Dot was really proud of herself. Beyond proud. She hadn't yet had a chance to check out the entire gym's worth of tables, but from what she had seen, the other entries were exactly as she'd predicted.

Mean Zelda Hooper had made the highly expected chart detailing the various types of fingerprints. She was offering "fingerprint reading" services, which was a bit like palm reading, on a much smaller scale. All of the "predictions," were, of course, mean. According to Zelda, "loops," the most common of the fingerprints, signified "low intelligence," an opinion she shared with the majority of the boys' soccer team. She also told Karyn Davis that the "whorl" on her middle finger meant that cutting her hair into bangs had been a mistake and also that nobody liked her.

In other news, Kevin Jones had built some sort of unimpressive battery. Shoko Harper had constructed a blobby model of the human brain. Most confusingly, Mo Baranski's project was reading tarot cards, which didn't seem very scientific at all.

Mr. Frang circled the gym, looking pensive. He was tall and thin and distinguished-seeming, with round eyeglasses and a semi-creepy gray goatee-style beard. Mr. Frang had a habit of petting his goatee whenever he was deep in thought, which appeared to be most of the time.

Dot did her best to read his expression as he visited each table. She knew Mr. Frang did his best to be diplomatic, but even so, she could tell he was not yet impressed with anyone's project.

Finally, he approached Dot's table.

"Well, Ms. Marino, what have we here?"

"I'm so glad you asked." Dot beamed. "This is a beehive coolant device."

This was her moment. She could basically taste the victory. Bask in the acclaim. Feel the heft of the weight of her first-place trophy as she held it in her hands.

"I see," Mr. Frang said, petting his goatee. "What is the optimal temperature for bees?"

"Bees are capable of working between fifty-seven and one hundred degrees Fahrenheit. They cannot fly if the temperature dips below fifty-five degrees, and if the temperature creeps above one hundred, they cluster and do not exert themselves in any way. Inside the hive, temperatures tend to hover between ninety and ninety-five degrees. The high temperature accounts for all of the activity taking place inside the hive, which of course generates energy and, thus, heat."

Dot was satisfied with her answer, but Mr. Frang looked dismayed. She had displayed such mastery of the subject of bees' ideal temperatures! Why wasn't he impressed?

Then she noticed. He was staring at the hive with a very quizzical expression.

Sure enough, the bees were moving slower than usual.

None of them were flying. And what was that? They appeared to be shivering. Dot hadn't even realized that bees could shiver. But these bees were doing exactly that.

"Uh-oh," she said softly. Her hive coolant device had performed very well during a recent test run. But today, it was performing a bit *too* well.

"The hive appears to be freezing," said Mr. Frang, concern saturating his voice.

"This whole gym is freezing!" yelled someone in the crowd.

"Turn off the air conditioning!" yelled Shoko, pulling her cardigan tightly around her body.

"Make it stop!" yelled Mo, from her tarot card table.

"Quick! Somebody get these bees a blanket!" yelled Mr. Frang.

None other than Pigeon sprang into action.

Of course, thought Dot.

"I've got it! Just a minute!" she called as she sprinted out of the gym. Dot just stood there, her mouth hanging open. Pigeon reappeared moments later, wielding one of the fire safety blankets they kept in the science lab, in case someone's experiment caught flame. She tossed it over Dot's table, covering the hive. Dot made a pathetic sound. With that one move, Pigeon had squashed both her project and her dreams.

A few people applauded. Dot had expected to hear applause, but for very different reasons. This was humiliating.

"Phew!" said Mr. Frang, panting, like he had personally averted a very stressful situation.

With that, he moved on to the next table, where Zephyr Strauss was all too happy to demonstrate how he had created bouncy balls out of glue and borax.

Inwardly, Dot panicked. That was NOT how she pictured things going. Her mom had been chasing her around the bungalow for the past week insisting that Dot's chakras were misaligned. Should she have listened? Had she brought this on herself?

Still, all wasn't lost. Her idea was a good one. Her technology was solid. She had just misfired a little bit. Surely she wouldn't be penalized for creating something that worked TOO well? Especially given all the predictable things on display all around her.

Then something made her stop cold.

"Wow!" she heard Mr. Frang exclaim.

"These are solar panels that anyone can attach to their vehicle."

"Incredible!" Mr. Frang said.

"Right now, they're optimized to work on vehicles with smaller engines, like electric scooters and bikes, but if this same technology were applied on a greater scale, it could work for a gas-powered vehicle, of any kind. With removable, rechargeable technology, this allows you to make some of your trips completely solar powered, greatly reducing your carbon footprint."

"So you can convert *any* gas-powered vehicle?" Mr. Frang asked.

"Yes!" Pigeon exclaimed, with glee.

WHAT? Dot nearly died. Pigeon had created WHAT?

Mr. Frang was taking photos. Dot had never seen him do that before. This was unprecedented.

Dot gripped the edge of the table. She thought she might faint.

How had this happened? What's more, how had Pigeon found the time to create such a stellar advancement with all the babysitting she'd been doing? Was she superhuman? This was all too much to handle.

"I think we may have a winner!" Mr. Frang exclaimed. Pigeon beamed. Dot suddenly felt nauseous.

Dot slowly made her way out of the gym and walked down

the hall to the girls' bathroom. She stood, resting her hands on the white porcelain sink, looking at her own reflection in the mirror.

LOSER was scrawled in blue marker on the tile wall in front of her. Dot's mom always said to look for signs from the universe, but this was honestly one sign she would have rather not seen. Dot had pictured this day for a long time, but in her daydreams, it had looked quite different. She barely recognized her life.

She had already given up babysitting, and now she had lost science, too.

CHAPTER TWENTY-FIVE

MALIA

At last, the blessed day had come.

It was the day Malia had been waiting for.

No, it was not the day of her wedding to Connor Kelly. No, she was not accompanying Connor to the middle school dance. No, she wasn't even going on a date or a walk or a previously specified hangout of any sort with Connor. NOT EVEN A GROUP ONE.

Still! It was the next best thing. It was the day of the Veronica concert. And Connor Kelly would be there.

Malia had — using a combination of mindfulness techniques that would surely make Dot's mom proud — finally shaken off the feeling of seeing him with Sage. So what if they'd gone to Marvelous Ray's? Everyone had been to Marvelous Ray's. So what if they'd gone together? After all, Connor had thought that Sage was Malia. How much of an impression could Sage really have made surrounded by all those blinking arcade lights?

Today was a new day. This was a new chapter. And Malia was ready.

After trying on every possible combination of clothes in her closet, Malia decided on—drumroll please—a striped T-shirt and jeans. Yes, it was a variation on what she always wore. But why fix what's not broken?

Bree arrived at the stadium looking like she was dressed up as a "Veronica fan" for Halloween.

She was wearing a black official Veronica tour T-shirt with *Veronica* printed all over it in red letters, red jeans, red sparkly sneakers just like the ones Veronica wore, and a red baseball hat covered in various Veronica pins. Her T-shirt had a giant slash on the right side, so her right sleeve dangled somewhere halfway down her arm, where the feline Veronica had tried to help out with styling.

"That's a lot of look," said Dot, who was wearing . . . black. Just like Dot always wore black. Nothing to see there.

"What if Veronica can see us from the stage?" Bree said, completely serious. "I want her to know how much I love her."

"I don't care if she can see us. I'm only going for the food," Dot announced, for what was probably the thirtieth time.

"We know, we know. You think Veronica is gimmicky and overrated and you're only excited about the carbohydrates," Malia said.

"Precisely," said Dot, who despite her words was clearly beaming with excitement. "I mean, I can't even believe I came to this."

The entry gates were down a long concrete staircase. As the girls made their way down the steps, Bree started to whine.

"Uh, you guys? I have to pee," Bree said.

"We can pee when we're inside the concert hall," said Malia. The plan was to get inside, find their seats, and then find out where Connor was, stat. Everything else could come later.

"It's kind of an emergency," said Bree.

"You sound like one of the kids we babysit for!" said Malia.

"It's probably just all the adrenaline from the concert," said Dot. "Not that I would know what that feels like."

"Can we just go around the side, to the porta potties?" Bree begged. She pointed to a sad line of porta potties that stood at the edge of the parking lot.

Malia and Dot both wrinkled their noses.

"There's, like, no line right now," Bree protested.

"There's a good reason there's no line," Malia said.

But the three of them begrudgingly trudged over toward the porta potties, because that's what friends do.

As they made their way to the far side of the parking lot, something shiny caught Malia's eye. A large black SUV had pulled up next to the building. It was at least ten yards away, behind a blockade of metal gates. Malia had a feeling she knew who was inside.

"Hey, guys," Malia said, pointing.

Everyone turned just in time to see the back doors open. Two very large men emerged from the SUV, followed by one very small lady. It was none other than Veronica.

She was wearing gray sweatpants with very, very high yellow heels and a black bomber jacket. It was the craziest outfit Malia had ever seen, but on Veronica, it worked.

"AHHHHHHHHHHHHHHHHHHHHH!" Bree screamed. It was easily heard on Mars.

"V-V-V-Veronica," Dot stammered.

Malia thought Veronica looked cool. She was much smaller in person than she seemed in videos. This was one of the top-three coolest things that had ever happened to her. Still, Malia

had to admit, seeing Veronica was, somehow, still not as excit-
ing as seeing Connor Kelly.

"I NAMED MY CAT AFTER YOU!" Bree shrieked.

Veronica turned to see where the outburst had come from.
Catching Bree's eye, Veronica made wild clawing motions at
the air, not unlike the feline Veronica. Then she winked before disappearing into the stage door, surrounded by her body-
guards.

"AHHHHHHHHHHHHHHHHHHHH!" Bree yelled
again.

Fully in a daze, the girls slowly made their way back toward
the entrance to the concert hall.

"I can't believe it!" Bree kept saying. "I can't believe it! I
can't believe it!"

"I thought you had to pee," said Dot.

"It went away," said Bree. "I can't believe it!"

At long last, they passed through security, squeezed their
way through the crowded entry gates, and into the Playa del
Mar Arts Center, which was a giant, open-air amphitheater surrounded by a park. In their town, any event worth going to always happened here. The opening act was already playing, some
smaller, up-and-coming band that Malia vaguely recognized.

"Ooh! Chicken fingers!" said Dot, making a beeline for a concession stand.

"Okay, so our tickets are in section D," said Malia, wishing she'd been able to ask Connor where his box was.

"This place is huge," said Bree, looking overwhelmed.

The crowd was something to behold. Veronica (the superstar, not the cat) had inspired everyone — from little kids with their parents to teenagers to full-fledged adults — to come out. Still, out of everyone around them, Bree was by far the most festively dressed.

"All right, I'm ready," said Dot, reappearing with a large basket of chicken fingers.

The girls trudged up a long set of stairs toward section D.

"WHERE is Connor?" Malia asked, looking all over the concert hall.

After climbing for what felt like forever, they arrived at section D. It was what some people would call the nosebleed section. It seemed they were almost in the clouds.

"Okay, these seats are not near anything," said Bree. "I dreamt that I might be able to reach out and touch Veronica while she was singing, even just one of her toes. But I don't think I could throw something at her from here."

Not only were they not close enough to the stage to touch

Veronica, they could barely *see* the stage. At best, Veronica would look like a tiny dot. Thank goodness they had at least gotten a glimpse of her earlier.

"WHERE is Connor?" Malia repeated. She had worked really hard for these tickets. She had worked really hard for this dream. She was not letting it go down as a story about a crowded night with some chicken fingers.

"This chicken finger is so good," said Dot.

At least someone was happy.

The opening band was just leaving the stage. After a few moments, the lights in the auditorium went completely black. The audience, Bree in particular, gave an excited scream.

The first few notes of the first song sounded. Malia immediately recognized it as "Selfie to My Soul," arguably Veronica's biggest hit. The crowd went wild.

In a huge flash, the spotlights came on at once, and Veronica herself appeared in the middle of the stage. She was dressed entirely in sequins. Bree looked like she might pass out.

The crowd danced wildly along with the song, which made it harder for Malia to see people's faces. Specifically Connor's.

"Take a selfie please. Say I'm everything," sang Dot. *"Make a memory, for eternity . . ."*

"I'm sorry, do you know ALL THE WORDS?" Malia couldn't believe it. "You're a closet fan!" she exclaimed.

"I am not!" Dot protested.

"You are. You love Veronica!" Malia had known it all along. Dot was less than amused.

"Everyone knows the words to this song, Malia," Dot grumbled. "They play it everywhere like every five minutes. That hardly makes me a fan." Still, she continued singing along.

"VERONICAAAAAAAA! I LOVE YOU!" Bree yelled. "YOU'RE MY FAVORITE PERSON! I'M THE ONE WHO NAMED MY CAT AFTER YOU!"

Finally, Malia saw him: her own personal version of the world's biggest superstar.

"There he is!" Malia pointed upward, where Connor Kelly was not quite dancing in a skybox. He was awkwardly bopping to and fro with a bunch of boys she recognized from school.

And also Sage.

"We have to go up there," Malia said, determination coloring her voice.

"Seriously?" said Dot. "You want to go up to that crowded box where it will be way too loud to talk to Connor anyway?" She squinted up at the box. Suddenly, her expression changed. "Wait a second. Is that Pigeon?"

"See? We have to get to that box!"

"Pigeon has friends?" Dot said, genuinely perplexed. "But she just moved here, and she isn't nice."

"I LOVE YOU, VERONICA!" Bree yelled.

"How does she have friends?" Dot asked.

"Let's go!" Malia screamed over the roar of the crowd.

The girls battled their way through the bopping concertgoers and up to the box containing Connor, Pigeon, and Sage. The sight of the satellite sitters had put a dark cloud over what was meant to be a very joyous occasion.

Sage's face lit up as soon as they entered the box. "So fun to see you here!" she yelled. Malia couldn't help but notice that Sage was dancing a little too close to Connor for Malia's comfort. "Did we ALL buy tickets with our babysitting money? How amazing is this?"

"Amazing," Malia said, but what she really meant was, "Terrible."

"How annoying is this?" Malia yell-whispered into Dot's ear.

"This can't continue," said Dot, who was eyeing Pigeon talking up a group of kids from school.

Pigeon's outfit was also black, but it was cooler somehow. Her button-down shirt had a complicated stud pattern all over the back, and her black jeans were perfectly fitted and ripped at the knees in just the right way. Even her sneakers looked dirty in an appealing way. Malia suddenly understood why Dot found her so irritating. She looked just like Dot, with a style upgrade.

"Hi, Connor!" said Malia. This was her moment. She was finally talking to Connor, at the concert. But the box was so crowded and loud that he just waved at her, with seven people standing in between them.

"Oh my god, you guys! It's my favorite song," said Bree.

"Which song is this?" said Dot.

"It's called 'Goodest Goodbye,'" said Malia. "Don't act like you don't know."

"Goodbye, goodbye, goodbye," sang Bree. *"It's time to say the goodest goodbye . . ."*

Yes, thought Malia. It was time to say goodbye . . . to the satellite sitters. It was time to take back their babysitting business and their lives. Her big idea had gotten them into this mess in the first place. Now she just needed a bigger idea to somehow get them out of it.

CHAPTER TWENTY-SIX

Dot

When Dot had agreed to host a sleepover at her house after the Veronica concert, she hadn't been aware that her mother would be hosting a full moon circle in the living room. As the girls opened the front door to the bungalow, they were surprised to discover twelve adults, all dressed in some version of flowing caftans, sitting in a circle on the floor.

Dot's mom sat in the center of the circle, perched atop a meditation cushion. Her frizzy red hair was even larger than usual, forming a voluminous halo that jutted out nearly a foot around her. She was playing her new favorite thing, a singing bowl—essentially a large glass bowl—while a man named Lyon (a regular at these gatherings) walked slowly around the perimeter of the room, waving a bundle of burning sage.

Oy, thought Dot.

Dot tried to walk quietly, hoping that she and her friends could make it back to her room unscathed. By now, her friends were used to Dot's mother's antics, but it never made it less embarrassing.

Unfortunately, before they were safely out of the living room, Malia tripped on the fringe of a very fringed carpet, causing her to stumble a bit. The moon worshippers looked up.

"Dot!" said her mother, the sounds of the singing bowl still reverberating in the air.

"Oh, hi there! We're just headed back to my room," said Dot. "Don't let us disturb you."

"Would you like to join us?" asked Lyon. Sage smoke wafted through the air around him, while no one said anything.

"Oh, that's so nice of you!" said Bree.

"But we really have to get going," added Dot.

"Official club business and all," added Malia.

"All right, then. You girls enjoy!" Dot's mom trilled as they scooted out of the living room as quickly as possible.

"Sorry about that," said Dot, closing her bedroom door behind her. The air inside had become tinged with sage smoke, and the singing bowl could still be heard echoing down the hall.

"Your mom's friends seem so fun," said Bree.

"They're fun the way a safari is fun," said Dot. "Best observed from a safe distance."

Malia nodded. "Makes sense."

"You guys, that was the most magical night!" Bree said, spinning in a dizzy circle and flopping back onto Dot's bed.

"Magical?" Malia scoffed. "That was depressing."

"Well, it was a mix of things," said Dot. "I think the word is 'conflicted.'"

"The satellite sitters are ruining everything!" Malia said as the sounds of some kind of chanting started up in the living room. "Tonight we experienced two of the most wonderful things on the planet—Veronica and Connor Kelly—at the same time. And it was still a messed-up experience."

"What would Veronica do?" Bree asked. "Person Veronica, I mean."

"Person Veronica would never get herself into this situation in the first place," Dot said. "I mean, at least that's how I imagine her."

"So what do we do?" Malia said.

"Can't we just fire them?" Bree asked. "Isn't that what un-happy bosses do?"

"No, because they're in too deep," Dot grumbled. "They've already taken all of our connections."

"Even our family members," added Bree.

"Yeah, and our clients like them a little too much. If we cut ties, the families could just hire them independently, and then they'd keep ALL the fees," Malia explained.

"Oh," said Bree. "That would be bad."

"We have to drive them out of babysitting altogether!" Malia said.

"But how do we do that?" asked Bree.

"We make their lives miserable," Malia said. "We show them how annoying babysitting can be, and also how nice life is *without* babysitting. And we start tomorrow."

"But Pigeon excels at babysitting," said Dot angrily. "The same way she excels at everything."

"Not for long," said Malia. "We're about to show them who's boss."

"Good, good, good goodbye," sang Bree.

"It's time to say the goodest goodbye," Malia chimed in.

"I'm better off without you, so now I can pursue my truth," Bree and

Malia sang together. Dot was slightly bopping her head along with them but wasn't chiming in.

"Oh COME ON, it's obvious you're a fan!" Malia said.

Dot smiled. She had tried so hard to hide it, but the jig was up. She had been found out.

"Good, good, good goodbye!" all three of them sang.

CHAPTER TWENTY-SEVEN

Bree

Where's the thing?" shouted Bree.

"Uhhhhhh, what thing?" asked Brody. He was genuinely perplexed.

"Brody. The thing! Where is it?" yelled Bree.

"Um, I'll try to find it," he said, and scurried off down the stairs.

"And take Veronica with you!" yelled Bree. Veronica was already following Brody before Bree had said anything, so she figured she might as well make it part of the command.

Bree turned to Malia. "Was that right?" she asked.

"That was good, but don't be afraid to be even angrier for no reason," coached Malia. "Like, if he returns without the thing, it's fine to go completely berserk."

"But that's so mean and crazy," said Bree. Yes, she wanted

Brody to quit so he could leave Bree and her family alone. But he was still a nice person. Bree felt terrible torturing him this way.

Malia just looked at her. "That's the point."

Their only hope was to turn the satellite sitters against babysitting altogether. But since Bree could be kind of a softie, Malia and Dot had come over to provide Bree with some backup. Since Malia had the most experience with horrible bosses, she was offering her expert advice.

As predicted, a few moments later, Brody poked his head in the bedroom door.

"I'm soooooo sorry, but I can't find the thing," he said. He stepped fully into the room, with Veronica at his ankles. "To be honest, I'm still not sure I know what the thing is."

"Are you still doing THAT?" said Malia. "We found the thing ages ago. Now we need you to go to the kitchen and count everything in the fridge and then everything in the freezer and then everything in the pantry and come back and tell us how many items are in each place. And do it as soon as possible."

"Okaaaaaay," said Brody in his lilting drawl. "But, um, why?"

"Because it's important!" said Malia. "And we need it done quickly. No time for questions!"

"All right," said Brody, and left the room.

Brody never outwardly showed any anxiety. He just moved slowly and methodically through his life, and ultimately got stuff done. Aside from the part where he stole her family, he was still a very good hire.

"What if this doesn't work?" asked Dot.

"Of course it will work, what kind of lunatic would stay in a job where they get yelled at all the time?" asked Malia.

"Um, you?" asked Bree.

"That's different. That's because my sister is the devil and my mom won't let me quit." Malia sighed. "As far as we know, Brody is just doing this for fun. As soon as we make it not fun, he will leave us."

"Maybe we should check on Bailey," said Bree, reasoning that doing something helpful would make her feel slightly better about tormenting Brody.

"He's watching a movie," said Dot.

"So? We can still see how he's doing," Bree pushed.

The girls went downstairs to find that Bailey was, indeed, watching a movie. The movie was about a very evil clown (Bree's actual nightmare), and he was extremely engrossed in it. He had zero interest in even saying hello to them.

With that, the girls headed to the kitchen to load more demands on Brody.

"Are you done counting?" yelled Malia.

"What's taking so long?" added Dot.

They entered the kitchen to find the pantry door open, with poor Brody rummaging around inside.

"There are forty-three things in the fridge, seventeen things in the freezer, and seventy-two things in the pantry," he called.

Bree trusted that he was capable of counting, but she opened the refrigerator door just to take a peek. She gasped. Brody had not only counted the contents of the fridge; he had cleaned and organized it as well. Bree never thought she could think such a thing about a kitchen appliance, but the fridge looked beautiful.

What? Malia mouthed, seeing Bree's reaction.

He's a wizard, Bree mouthed back.

Bree peeked into the pantry. Veronica was curled sweetly near Brody's feet, napping. It was in that moment Bree realized she had never seen Veronica nap before. Again, she was forced to think that Brody was some kind of magic being.

Brody was in the process of organizing every item in the

pantry first by category and then by color. The pantry was well on its way to being the most gorgeous storage facility Bree had ever seen.

"Wow," Bree said. "We only needed you to count the items, not make it look like a snack museum."

"Oh, it only takes a second and, like, makes such a big difference. You know?" Brody said.

"Where did you learn how to do that?" she asked.

Brody just shrugged.

What a mysterious person, thought Bree. She realized that even though he was in the process of taking over her home and her family, she actually knew very little about him.

Bree hurried out of the kitchen, motioning for her friends to join her.

"What do we do?" she asked. "He's not quitting. He's going above and beyond."

"Maybe he should go work for Ramona," said Malia.

"This is a very unexpected turn of events," said Dot.

"Maybe I should just give up," said Bree. "He's too good. He's better at everything."

"No," said Malia. "Never give up. We just need to change tactics."

Bree wasn't so sure. Maybe she could learn to adjust to life with her new brother Brody. In exchange for relinquishing her place in her family, she would at least get a calm cat and very clean cabinets. She tried to imagine this for a moment, but it still made her sad.

No, Bree thought, shaking her head. That would never do. After all, what good were clean cabinets if you didn't have a family to enjoy their contents with? What good was a calm cat if it was practically the only mammal who ever paid attention to you?

There was only one way forward. Brody had to go.

CHAPTER TWENTY-EIGHT

MALIA

Malia had her eyes on the prize.

But someone was standing in the way of that prize, and that person was Sage.

Malia was loitering at her locker, pretending to get ready for homeroom, but really, she was spying on Sage. Normally, Malia liked to spend her mornings watching for Connor, as it was the most positive way to start the day. But lately, even that beloved pastime had felt less enjoyable, because Sage was always standing in her eye line, talking to some boy.

Malia watched as Sage hung her jacket up in her locker. As usual, boys surrounded her, like ants on a crumb. How did she manage to be so sociable so early in the morning? Malia hadn't even eaten breakfast yet. She barely knew what her own name was, and yet, there was Sage, talking to, like, seven boys at once. It was almost a talent.

Malia saw Bree coming down the hallway and waved her over.

"Let's go talk to Sage," Malia said. "It's time to put our plan in action."

"Okay!" said Bree, then immediately followed it up with, "What plan?"

"The plan where we somehow convince her to give up babysitting," said Malia.

"Oh, right."

"We'll just go over there and act like we have to talk about official babysitting business," said Malia, leading the way. "And then I'll make her realize she needs to quit."

"Sounds good!" Bree said, following behind.

Malia leaned next to Sage's open locker, causing a couple of the surrounding boys to clear away.

"Oh, hi, Sage," Malia said casually, as though she hadn't come over with the express purpose of talking to her.

"Hi, guys! How's it going?"

"We wanted to talk to you about some very official babysitting business," said Bree.

"Stealth," whispered Malia under her breath. She looked down the hallway, where Connor was taking a drink from the water fountain. "Oh man," she said. "Isn't it so annoying how Connor Kelly always wears a different version of, like, the exact same thing every single day?" She motioned toward Connor, who was rummaging in his own locker.

As soon as the words escaped her mouth, she felt like a traitor. In truth, Malia loved that Connor wore the same thing — a solid crew-neck T-shirt and perfectly fitting jeans — every day. She thought it pointed to a man who was consistent, a seventh-grader who knew who he was and what he liked at a precociously early age. His uniform also made it easy for Malia to daydream about him, as his appearance was always consistent.

"Um, I've never really thought about it," said Sage. "In fact, I hadn't really noticed before."

LIES! thought Malia.

"I mean, we wear the same thing almost every day, too," said Sage, pointing to her own striped T-shirt.

Hm. She kind of had a point. Malia decided to change tactics.

"You know what else is annoying? Babysitting," said Malia.

Sage looked confused for a minute.

"SO ANNOYING," Bree chimed.

"You know what I mean? Like when you really want to just hang out with your friends and have fun and go to the mall and maybe talk to a cute boy? But instead you have to hang out with children who are cute but definitely not in the same way that boys are?"

Sage looked thoughtful for a moment. Malia hoped she was considering the weight of this very important question.

"No," said Sage. "If anything, babysitting is actually the perfect job if you like boys, because it sometimes lets you interact with them! Like when the kids have cute boys for neighbors or when the kids have cute older cousins or something." This was not going the way Malia wanted. Sage continued. "And it lets me earn money so I can hang out with friends at the mall or the arcade or whatever. And there are always boys at those places."

I KNOW, thought Malia. THAT IS WHY I WANT MY JOB BACK.

"But also, aren't the kids so annoying sometimes?" Malia pressed on.

Once again, Sage looked thoughtful. "No. You know, I expected it to be harder. But it's, like, once you get to know their individual personalities, kids are actually really fun!"

Ugh. This was going to be harder than she realized.

"You know who looks really cute lately?" said Malia, trying one final tactic.

Bree shot her a confused look. The babysitting portion of the conversation was definitely over.

"Aidan Morrison," said Sage.

"Yes!" said Malia. "He's been wearing his hair differently."

"It really suits him," gushed Sage.

"Oh, totally," agreed Malia.

Malia really didn't care for Aidan Morrison or his new haircut. Malia didn't really care for any of the other boys in the grade. It was annoying how Sage's love spread across all boys. Why couldn't she just leave Connor alone? She didn't even appreciate his uniqueness, so why should she take up his attention?

"Hey," said a voice. It was THE voice. The voice of Connor.

Had Malia's thoughts summoned him over?

"Oh, hey!" said Malia, like she hadn't just been thinking about him.

Now would be the perfect time to ask him about the concert. But before she could speak, Sage started making words.

"Are you on your way to homeroom?" asked Sage.

"Yeah," said Connor.

What was this?

"Great! I'm headed that way," said Sage.

"Bye, Malia," said Sage and Connor, in unison, as they walked down the hallway, in the opposite direction of Malia's own homeroom.

This was much worse than Malia had thought. She had to get Sage to quit babysitting, but even more pressingly, she had to get Sage to quit Connor. Or else Malia was going to have to quit everything.

CHAPTER TWENTY-NINE

Dot

"Of course it will work," said Malia with what sounded to Dot like a bit too much confidence.

"Just like it worked with Sage and Brody," said Dot.

"Those plans are *in progress*," Malia said defensively. "They haven't not worked. Good things take time."

"Mm-hmm," said Dot. "Whatever you say."

The girls were gathered in Dot's room for an official club meeting. But instead of discussing the usual business topics — upcoming jobs, fees, scheduling — they were entirely focused on what to do about the new hires. Namely Pigeon de Palma.

"You just love making fake email accounts any chance you can get," said Dot.

"Because it works!" said Malia. She stopped to think for a moment. "Although I guess that's technically how Ramona found her way into my life, so maybe I should be more careful about these things."

Indeed, the last time Malia made a fake email account, it was to convince Chelsea that Ramona Abernathy, who at the time meant nothing more to her than a wealthy town figure, was interested in hiring an experienced babysitter. Malia wrote a fake email from "Ramona" and sent it to Chelsea. As it turned out, Ramona wasn't looking for a babysitter, but she was looking for an intern, and the rest was history.

Malia tapped her keyboard. "Okay, so who should this email be from? A senator? A famous scientist?"

"No, Pigeon already interned for Elon Musk last summer," said Dot, rolling her eyes. "Let's make it from the director of a fake science program that's too good to pass up. From like, Johns Hopkins or MIT or something."

"What's that?" asked Bree.

"A really smart school for science people," said Malia.

"One of the top universities in the country for science and technology," said Dot.

"Literally what I said," said Malia. She started typing. "Okay, so we'll say it's from MIT Youth Talent Recruitment."

"Yes! And they should invite her to apply for a really advanced program that, like, nobody gets into," Dot said.

"Perfect!" said Bree, absently petting Veronica with one hand. Veronica was securely in his carrier, as always, but Bree had opened the door just enough to squeeze one of her hands in. Veronica looked perturbed, like he was barely tolerating the human contact.

"Dear gifted scientific youth," Malia read out loud as she typed.

"They would never say that." Dot crossed her arms.

"Okay, fine, then you tell me what to type. It can be just like when Ramona makes me do 'dictation.' I am just your lowly typist," said Malia.

"Dear Ms. De Palma," Dot recited. "It is my great pleasure to invite you to participate in the MIT Summer Scholars Program for Gifted and Talented Youth."

"That's good," said Bree.

"Meow," said Veronica.

"This letter goes out to a very select group of students who have demonstrated above-average academic abilities," Dot continued as Malia typed.

"I wish I got letters like that," Bree said softly.

"This email isn't real," Malia reminded her. "No one gets letters like this."

"In order to gain entry into this very exclusive and

prestigious program, we ask that you build a solar-powered rocket. The rocket can be to your own specifications, using any parts you wish. We only ask that the rocket is completely constructed by you and is capable of remaining in flight for a minimum of two hundred and forty seconds."

"This sounds really complicated," said Bree.

"She'll totally do it," said Malia. "I bet she'll drop everything and spend all her time building this rocket to nowhere. And then you can win at life."

"We look forward to receiving your submission and are even more excited about the prospect of welcoming you to our gifted and talented program this summer."

"Who should we sign it from?" asked Malia.

"Mildred Kittersberg," said Dot.

"Who's that?" asked Bree.

Dot just shrugged. "Sounds uptight and sciencey."

"Great!" said Malia, pressing Send.

The email was on its way out the door. Dot could only hope that Pigeon was right behind it.

Historically, Dot always sat with the honors kids at lunch, but ever since Pigeon came onto the scene, everything had changed. The other kids hung on her every braggy word

("Why yes, I do have Sheryl Sandberg's direct contact in my cell phone! My dad knows her personally!"), and it was too much for Dot to stomach. So for the time being, she'd taken to sitting with Malia and Bree and Shoko and Mo at their less pretentious lunch table.

"Do you know if Pigeon got the email yet?" Malia asked through a mouthful of peanut butter.

"I mean, I'm sure she got the email. We sent it yesterday, so she got it yesterday. That is how emails work," said Dot.

"But do we know if she's, like, building her impossible rocket?" Bree asked.

"We can only hope," said Dot.

"Or we can follow up," said Malia.

"How?" asked Bree.

"We cannot ask her," Dot said. Malia had that look on her face like she always got when she was scheming, and it was making Dot nervous.

Malia grabbed Dot's phone. Before Dot could object, Malia started yelling.

"Oh my God!" Malia exclaimed at a volume more appropriate for a stadium than a lunchroom. "Dot, YOU GOT AN EMAIL FROM THE MASSACHUSETTS INSTITUTE OF

TECHNOLOGY?" Malia was not a good actor. She sounded like she was reading lines from a very bad play.

"Shh, you're being embarrassing." Dot covered her face with her hands. It was bad enough she was sitting at a different lunch table, but now she was also becoming a spectacle.

"WOW!" Bree joined in the charade.

"WOW, THAT SOUNDS SO PRESTIGIOUS," Malia continued.

Pigeon looked up.

"It's working," Malia singsong-whispered.

"You're ruining my life," Dot groaned, her hands still covering her face.

But sure enough, Pigeon was coming to investigate.

"What's all this about an email?" she asked.

"Oh, Dot here just got a very impressive-sounding email from MIT," said Malia.

"I got that, too," Pigeon said, waving a hand dismissively. "It wasn't real."

"What are you talking about?" said Dot, feeling suddenly invested in the scheme.

"It's from some bogus account. Haven't you ever heard of phishing?" Pigeon laughed.

"Like the band?" said Bree.

"You guys are so funny," said Pigeon. "Did you think that email was real? It was from some weird dot com. Any correspondence from the real MIT would have come from a dot edu."

"Obviously," said Dot, trying to save herself. "I didn't get a good look at the email address because Malia grabbed my phone."

Malia shot her a look.

"It's too bad the email was fake, though," said Pigeon wistfully. "It said applicants were being asked to build a solar-powered rocket, and I'm actually taking Aloysius to the Museum of Science this weekend to look at an exhibit about that exact thing!"

Dot fought the urge to launch her chicken finger, rocket-style, right at Pigeon's face.

"Oh well, see you later," said Pigeon, turning so swiftly that the chicken finger would never have had a chance.

With that, Pigeon sauntered off.

CHAPTER THIRTY

MALIA

Gym class. More torture than class. At least, as far as Malia was concerned.

Today, Coach K had decided all of the seventh-graders should practice the long jump. He set up shop in the huge sand pit running along one side of the track. The students were expected to get a running start and then take a flying leap over the sandpit. This was a horrible idea for many reasons.

Why was this a necessary skill in life? Malia wondered. Unless one encountered a very large puddle and also couldn't walk around it, when would a person ever need to do the long jump?

That's why Bree, Dot, and Malia were safely situated on the opposite side of the field, as far away as they could possibly be from the sand pit. They were sitting in the bleachers—okay, technically, they were sitting under the bleachers, which could also be characterized as hiding.

"This whole thing is a liability," said Dot, staring down the field, where Francine Fitzmeyer had just taken a flying flop into the sandpit, where she landed right on her face. "Look at poor Francine. She's going to feel bad about this for at least a week."

"You just hate everything to do with this school since the science fair happened," said Malia.

"Next up, Pigeon de Palma!" yelled Coach K.

The timing was uncanny.

Pigeon sped down the track and leaped into the air, like some sort of gazelle. Naturally, she cleared the entire sandpit, landing gracefully on the far end of it.

"UGH! Look at her," said Dot, not even trying to hide her contempt.

"How do you really feel?" asked Malia.

"It's just, like, why is she trying to be good at everything? Who does she think she is?" Dot said.

"You," Malia responded. "I think she thinks she's you. She thinks she can be super smart and good at every subject but especially science and sit with the honors kids at lunch. She thinks she can win prizes and also babysit in her free time.

She hasn't yet realized that there already was a you and she's stepping on your toes."

"But even I don't care about being good at *gym*," Dot spat. "She's outdoing me! Why can't she just be good at gym? Why does she have to step all over my turf?"

"At least she isn't practically living at your house and taking over your family," said Bree. "Brody stole my brother! Brody stole my parents!"

There was a long silence as the girls stared wistfully out at the field.

"We should never have hired them," Malia conceded. "I miss the old days, when the club was our main focus. I can't tell if the new sitters have been too good at taking our places, or if we let them win too easily."

"It all seemed like a good idea at first," Dot said, "But as it turns out, this might have been the worst one yet."

Malia watched as Sage, wearing the exact same gym outfit as her (cropped leggings, tank top) in a slightly darker shade of blue, made her running start. But just as she approached the sand pit, her nerves seemed to get the better of her. She stopped short, just as it was time to jump.

"Sorry!" she said, shrugging helplessly. But instead of

thinking she was a failure, everyone seemed to think it was funny.

"That's totally something I would do," said Malia. "In fact, I've done it before. But when I do it, no one laughs. When Sage does it, everyone thinks it's cute."

"Let's face it," Dot said. "We basically hired doppelgangers of ourselves."

"Dopplerwhats?" asked Bree.

"Doppelgangers," Dot repeated. "It's like, a double, or a long-lost twin. Consciously or unconsciously, we picked three people who are weirdly similar to us."

Bree digested this information for a moment.

"Wait—does that mean my twin is Brody?" Bree seemed offended. "I do NOT look like Brody."

"You definitely don't," Malia agreed. "But you're, like, spirit doppelgangers."

"You guys do have similar mannerisms sometimes," Dot argued.

"And you're both so sweet," Malia said. "And he does have a way with animals . . ." She trailed off before Bree could become annoyed. Although, come to think of it, Bree didn't really get annoyed. And neither did Brody.

"And Sage is your spirit doppelganger because she loves Connor!" Bree said.

"She loves ALL boys," Malia clarified. Still, the thought made her grimace.

"So how do we get rid of them?" Bree asked. "We've already tried, and they won't go away!"

"We must take our lives back," Malia said. She felt so impassioned that she stood up, although she could only stand eighty percent of the way so she wouldn't hit her head on the bleachers. "Dot's point is a good one. We hired doppelgangers. Which is a little weird, honestly, and kind of concerning. But! No matter. We must use this to our advantage."

"How do we do that?" Bree wondered.

"Well, since we're basically dealing with versions of ourselves, it's almost like we have insider knowledge. We must do some deep self-examination. What are our greatest weaknesses? What are our biggest fears? What are the things that we fear could destroy us?"

"Cats?" Bree ventured.

"Deeper than that," Malia said.

"Clowns?" Bree tried again.

"More internal," Malia said. "We have to face the things

that shake us to the core. We need to gain mastery over who we really are. Only then can we summon the strength to take back what's ours."

"How do we do that?" asked Bree.

A very valid question. Malia wasn't completely sure how they would accomplish this. They couldn't fire the doppelgangers. And thus far, their efforts to force them to quit had failed. But maybe they could beat them at their own game.

"Maybe it's not just about exploiting what we're afraid of," Dot said. "Maybe the key to winning against the doppelgangers isn't to hinge on what they don't like, but also to focus on what they love."

Malia nodded. She wasn't yet sure how their plan would come together, but she knew that it would. Sage loved boys more than babysitting. Brody loved animals and people. Pigeon loved glory and recognition. Maybe these were the keys to take down the doppelgangers and take back their jobs, once and for all.

CHAPTER THIRTY-ONE

Dot

Dot was sad. There was no other way around it. She had such high hopes, and thanks to Pigeon, they had all been dashed.

After Malia's speech in gym class, Dot had hung around after school. She felt too listless to move quickly, too depressed to seek out another activity. She had nowhere to go. Instead, she waited until everyone else had cleared out of the building, and then she walked slowly down the halls.

She stopped when she got to the gymnasium, where the science fair projects were still set up on display. She knew she shouldn't go inside, but she couldn't help herself. It was like visiting the scene of a crime. She couldn't stop herself from looking away.

The hive was still on its table, the bees buzzing away despite (or perhaps because of) the fact that her losing device had been turned off. Dot continued to make a lap around the gym, running her hand wistfully along the edge of each table. It just wasn't fair. So many of these experiments were phoned in. They weren't even trying to be innovative. Shouldn't she at least have gotten credit for trying? So what if the execution was a little flawed? Her idea was a good one, and with a little adjustment, maybe it really could save the world.

Still, they didn't give out Nobel Prizes for trying. Dot hadn't saved the world. She hadn't even saved a bunch of bees. She had just made them cold.

Dot knew it wasn't a crime that she had miscalculated the voltage of the hive coolant device and made it work a little too well. Good scientists—heck, good people—made mistakes all the time. Making mistakes was part of being a person. It wasn't simply losing the science fair that bothered her; it was losing to Pigeon.

Now Pigeon's name would adorn the plaque in the science lab where the winner's names had been recorded for as long as the school had been standing. She would get to compete at the regional science fair. She might even take Dot's place as Mr. Frang's favorite student.

Dot pulled the pyrite stone her mom had given her out of her pocket.

"Some good you did," she said.

Dot wasn't used to being shown up, especially when it came to academic endeavors. Sure, in some sweeping, philosophical way, she understood that the world was a very big place and there were people out there who were more talented, more driven, simply better than her. But until now, she had never encountered it before.

She didn't just feel like she was losing the science fair. She felt like she was losing her place at Playa del Mar. Her identity was all wrapped up in what made her different.

She ran her thumb over the pyrite stone.

The science fair may have been lost, but she wasn't prepared to give up everything else. Maybe, Dot thought, she should take back all the Aloysius jobs. She didn't need to work on the science fair anymore, so she could easily make the time. Plus, if Pigeon was left babysitting other kids, she would realize how much harder it was, and maybe it would drive her to quit. Other kids were rambunctious and loud and gross and incapable of independent scientific research. Babysitting Aloysius, on the other hand, was like having a real peer, even a confidant.

And that's when she made the connection. How hadn't she

realized it sooner? The solar panels that made Pigeon's project so revolutionary—they were just like what Aloysius would call "sustainable solar technology." This wasn't an original idea at all. It was a great idea—a winning idea—but it also wasn't Pigeon's.

Dot couldn't believe she hadn't seen it before. But the important thing was, she saw it now.

She took off running.

"Yes. Of course it's my idea! Along with the technology behind it. All of it is completely mine!" Aloysius waved his hands around as he spoke. "I've been working on this for weeks, months, even."

Dot had known the idea belonged to Aloysius, and now he had confirmed it. She thought back on the conversation they'd had that day as they walked to the library, when he had said he'd been working on solar-powered everything.

"I thought I was tutoring her!" Aloysius put his hand over his mouth in shock.

"Wait, you thought you were WHAT?" Dot couldn't believe her ears.

"She told me she needed a science tutor. She did a very good job seeming like she wasn't very academically gifted. I mostly felt bad for her. I had no idea she was stealing from me! Not to mention compromising your place in the fair in the process." He shook his five-year-old head in dismay. "This is terrible! I'm so sorry."

"No, I'm so sorry! I'm sorry we ever hired her, I'm sorry I let her watch you, I'm sorry you got caught up in this whole mess." Dot couldn't believe she had trusted her favorite baby-sitting charge with a cheating liar.

"I don't mean to make an already terrible situation more complicated, but I don't really like Pigeon," Aloysius said. "I mean, she's okay enough. Or she seemed okay enough, before I knew about all this. But she isn't you."

Dot was touched. "I've missed spending time together," she said.

"Me too!" Aloysius agreed. "So what are you going to do now?"

Dot smiled. "I think it's time for a comeback."

"Pigeon, may I see you for a moment?" Mr. Frang said.

Science class had just ended, and the rest of the students were gathering up their bags and funneling out into the hall-way. Dot moved very slowly, hoping to get a glimpse of the action.

Pigeon made her way to the front of the classroom, tossing her long, wavy hair over her shoulder. "Yes, Mr. Frang?" she said, cheerful as could be. Clearly, she had no idea what was about to go down.

Dot couldn't breathe.

At this point, pretty much all of the other students had left the classroom, so Dot had no choice but to file out behind them. She loitered near the outside of the science room door, pretending to be transfixed by a poster advertising an upcoming pep rally.

Dot held her breath as she watched them talk. She could feel her heart beating in her ears. She wasn't sure why she felt this way, since she wasn't the one getting in trouble. Sure, she had put the wheels in motion. She had gotten to school early enough to put the note on Mr. Frang's desk. It spelled out everything: where Pigeon had gotten her information and how she had framed it as her own. It included a copy of a report Aloysius had compiled for his mini MENSA camp, using the exact same technology Pigeon had tried to pass off as hers.

Dot should have felt happy, and on some level she guessed she did, but it was a conflicted kind of happiness. She didn't like getting people in trouble, but Pigeon had stolen from Aloysius, and that upset Dot even more than losing had. It wasn't right.

Mr. Frang was speaking too softly to make out what was going on, but she could tell that it wasn't going well for Pigeon. Her shoulders slumped a little bit more with each passing second. Finally, Pigeon turned and huffed out of the room, holding back tears.

Dot pretended to be involved in something on her phone, but Pigeon could still tell she'd been trying to eavesdrop.

"I know this is all because of you," she hissed, squinting at Dot as she passed. "I don't want anything to do with you, or your club, or this entire school. I hope you're happy."

As she watched Pigeon stalk off down the hallway, Dot finally exhaled a sigh of relief. She wasn't happy, exactly, at how it had all turned out, but she did feel redeemed. Sometimes, that was the most you could ask for.

CHAPTER THIRTY-TWO

Bree

Bree had practiced her speech in front of the mirror approximately seventy-three times. (First, she had tried to practice it by pretending Veronica was Brody, but that hadn't gone so well. She kept getting interrupted by violent outbursts and eventually had been forced to clean up the remains of the plastic display case that once housed her glitter nail polish.) She had thought and thought and thought and thought about the best way to make Brody quit. But finally, she realized, if someone was doing something that made her upset, she would want them to talk to her about it.

Bree had tried this approach with Veronica, and given the part where he didn't speak English and she didn't speak Cat, it had gone kind of meh so far. But when it came to Brody, Bree was hopeful they could have a heart-to-heart. She wasn't a fan of awkward conversations, but she understood that sometimes they were necessary. By now, she supposed she felt as ready as she would ever be.

It was simple, really. She just had to say: "Hey, Brody, you're obviously cool and all, but can you not steal my family? Thanks." But, like, maybe a little bit nicer than that. She hoped her anger wouldn't get the better of her. Most of all, she hoped that he would understand.

Brody lived in Playa del Norte, which was a ten-minute walk to the next town over. The quickest route was mostly along the boardwalk, the houses growing bigger and nicer with every passing block. Bree used this time to rehearse her speech yet again.

"They're my family!" she exclaimed at one point, slightly louder than she meant to.

An old man sat on a nearby bench, feeding the seagulls. He gave her a funny look. Bree just scurried away.

Bree hoped she would feel ready by the time she arrived at Brody's door. But here she was, at 78 Laurel Lane, and she still felt completely anxious. Her nerves weren't helped by the fact that Brody apparently lived in a castle. How was no one aware of this? Bree had thought her house was big, but it was nothing compared to this. Brody's front yard was so big it had actual gates in front of it, big enough for cars to drive through.

Smitherington, read a plaque on the gate. With a gasp, Bree realized she had never even known this was Brody's last name. He was basically part of her family now, yet she barely knew anything about him.

Bree walked through the gates, feeling sort of silly that she was just a person, not a car. She continued up the gravel driveway, her feet crunching with every step. The walk up the lawn felt almost as long as the walk to Playa del Norte. Finally, she reached the front door.

Bree rang the bell. It sounded loud and a little bit scary, like church bells. She waited.

She couldn't help but think of the first time she met Brody, when he wandered confusedly into their interviews and asked if they were selling Girl Scout cookies. Bree wished she were standing on this step to sell Girl Scout cookies. That would be a much easier conversation.

The door opened, and a very thin, very blond woman peered down at her.

"Good afternoon. Um, is Brody home?"

The woman looked at Bree as though she were speaking Swahili.

"I'm sorry, dear. Are you sure you have the right house?"

"Oh. Does Brody not live here?" Bree pulled out her phone so she could check the address.

"Bro-deeee?" The woman thought for a moment. "Are you referring to Brodford?"

"Who?"

"Brodford! Brodford Smitherington the Fourth? My elder son."

Before Bree could respond, Brody's familiar face appeared in the vestibule. But nothing else about him looked familiar. He was dressed in khaki slacks, a navy-blue sport jacket, a white button-down shirt, and a blue bow tie. He looked like he had just escaped from the nearest country club. He did not—in any way—resemble Brody.

"Whoa," said Bree.

"I've got this, Mom," said Brody.

His mom seemed skeptical about leaving her son alone with a strange, glittery girl, but after a long pause she reluctantly stepped away.

"What are you wearing?" Bree asked. "And *what* is your name?"

"Bree! Why are you here?" Even Brody's voice sounded different than usual. He spoke at a quick clip, any trace of his surfer vibe completely missing.

"I wanted to talk to you about . . . some stuff." Bree was already losing her nerve. "But now I discovered you have a secret life."

Brody glanced around nervously, making sure the coast was clear before he continued speaking.

"I can explain. Honestly, my life is . . . not very fun. You know I go to Fratford Academy, which is really intense." Bree nodded. "My entire life is, like, doing homework and having my parents get mad at me if I get anything less than an A. That's why I wanted to babysit. It was the most random thing, but it was a break from being me. It's so different than what I normally do. I got to be the one in charge! Plus, I could wear whatever I want and just act like a regular kid."

"Yeah, that must have been like a vacation for you," said Bree. She couldn't imagine what Brody's regular life was like. But she did love vacations.

"That's why I liked hanging out at your house," Brody said. "Your family is so big and loud and nice. Your parents don't care how anyone is dressed or if you know which fork is for salad."

Bree had no idea there was a fork especially for salad. Wasn't there just one type of fork?

"Oh," was all Bree could manage. Looking at this Brodford person, with his bow tie and his frighteningly high expectations, Bree felt bad for Brody. She had come here to tell him to back off her family, but now she wanted to invite him to move in. "I'm sorry," Bree said. "I didn't know any of that."

"Anyway, my mom got super mad at me the other day, because I got an A-minus in algebra. I guess all the time I've been spending babysitting took my focus away from my schoolwork, and my grades slipped. She's watching me like a hawk, so I don't think I'll be able to help you guys out anymore."

"Oh," Bree said again. This was technically good news. She was getting exactly what she wanted without having to ask for it. But Bree felt bad. It was the kind of bad she felt back in fourth grade when everyone thought the class rabbit had been kidnapped. Afraid for the safety of someone smaller and sadder and potentially in danger, but also not sure what else you could do to help. (As it turned out, the class rabbit was just hiding behind one of the bookshelves. But the feeling lived on.)

"I'll miss you guys," said Brody or Brodford or whoever he was.

"You're welcome to hang out with us, both the club and my family, whenever you want," Bree said.

"Thanks," said Brody. "I'd like that."

"Me too," said Bree. She was surprised to realize she actually meant it.

CHAPTER THIRTY-THREE

MALIA

Something is very wrong here!" Ramona yelled from inside her office.

These were the worst types of exclamations. Ramona loved to yell things like "Oops!" or "Uh-oh!" or "Oh-no!" or, simply, "HELP!" All of these had the ability to send Malia into panic mode before she had any idea what she was being asked to fix.

Today, the problem was with Ramona's coffee.

"There is too much coconut milk in this latte." Ramona sighed. "I like the color to be closer to a groundhog. A deep, golden brown. The color of this latte is closer to a camel."

This woman was absolutely bananas.

"Would you like me to make it again?" Malia asked.

"Yes. Please. And keep in mind this time: groundhog."

Malia picked up the mug and headed toward the kitchen.

She made another latte, using Ramona's fancy Italian coffee machine. Reasoning it was better to be safe than sorry, she actually googled a picture of a groundhog to make sure the color was accurate. (Though, in her own defense, even the Internet was aware that groundhogs were not necessarily uniform in color.)

When Malia returned just moments later, latte in hand, she found Ramona slumped over with her head resting on the desk. At first, Malia thought she might have died, but then Ramona let out a wail.

"Oh my. I'm sorry," she said, smoothing her hands over her helmet of perfectly groomed hair. "That wasn't very professional of me."

Like you've ever been concerned with acting professional, Malia thought.

"It's just that since my daughter moved to Playa del Norte, she's been expecting so much of me. Like she thinks I'm some regular retiree who has time to show her around town and point out the organic grocery stores and shop with her at Bed Bath and Beyond." Ramona rolled her eyes. "Not to mention she somehow expects me to entertain Martin. Like he has any interest in tootling around town with his grandmother."

"Is there anything I can do to help?" asked Malia. It was a rhetorical question. After all, Malia's job was already to help, and Ramona had no trouble asking her to do anything under the sun, appropriate and otherwise. But Ramona's face lit up at the suggestion.

"You know, I think there is something!" she said.

After just one hour together, Malia felt like she knew all there was to know about Ramona's grandson, Martin. The main thing was he was super, super hot. If one tried to measure his hotness, it would be a number so high it would take many hours to write it out. And if one tried to measure his intelligence, well, that number would not be so high.

So far, Martin had mistaken a squirrel for a cat. He had called Malia "Monica" no less than three times. Next, he proceeded to talk about his favorite sneakers and his favorite ice cream flavor (mint chocolate chip) for the better part of an hour. Martin was sweet, but his endless chatter made Malia yearn for the awkward silences normally supplied by other boys her age. She simply couldn't take it anymore.

Despite the original plan to give Martin the grand tour of Playa del Mar, Malia felt it was above and beyond her duties to suffer through any more time with him. So she decided the best thing to do was to find Martin his very own babysitter. One who would appreciate him.

Malia had been racking her brain for how to get Sage to quit. *What would make me quit?* Malia had wondered. Maybe she could use the same logic on Sage. But the more she thought about it, the more Malia realized that nothing would make her quit. Sometimes she could get frustrated, yes, or sometimes she might change course, but quitting wasn't in her DNA. She didn't give up—not on babysitting, not on Connor, not on anything she cared about.

And that's when Malia realized: Sage wasn't her doppel-ganger after all. Sage might like striped shirts and cute boys, but that's all they had in common. Because Sage had a short attention span. Malia reasoned all she had to do was distract her with a cute enough carrot, and run away.

Then, the universe had given her Martin.

"Is this the mall?" asked Martin as they approached the Gregory house.

Malia looked at him to see if he might be joking, but unfor-tunately he was completely serious. Malia sighed. He really was gorgeous from every single angle. (Every angle, that is, except inside his brain.)

Malia rang the doorbell, and as she had hoped, Sage answered right away.

At the sight of Martin, Sage's face lit up. If she were a cartoon, her eyes would have bugged out of her head. Malia knew that look. It was the same look she had given Connor every day since the dawn of time. (Or third grade. Which was basically the same thing.)

"Oh, hi, Sage," Malia said, as if she had just randomly stumbled up the Gregory family's front walkway. She hoped she sounded casual, as though she hadn't planned on this all along. "What are you up to?"

"Oh, you know. Babysitting," Sage said, never taking her eyes off Martin.

"Oh, Sage, I'd like you to meet someone. This is Martin Abernathy Pratt." Malia had always thought there was something about saying full names that made people seem more appealing. Not that such a thing was necessary in this particular instance.

"H-h-h-hi!" squeaked Sage.

"I was just showing Martin around Playa del Mar. You know, the mall, Marvelous Ray's, stuff like that," Malia said.

"Oh, really?" Sage said, totally taking the bait. "That sounds like SO much fun."

"Oh, it is," said Malia. "Basically the most fun."

Sage frowned.

"Too bad you have to babysit," said Malia, really driving the point home.

"I know. I really wish I could join you."

"The mall!" said Martin, somewhat inexplicably.

"Oh my god, you know what? I have an idea," said Malia, like she hadn't been plotting this exact moment.

"You do?" said Sage, hinging on Malia's every word.

"Yes. So, like, I have a ton of homework, and the full tour could take a long time. Sage, would you be comfortable showing Martin around without me?"

Sage looked like she might explode with enthusiasm.

"Of course. I mean, yes. I mean, I'd love to." Then her face fell again. "But what about babysitting?"

"Oh, that's no problem. I can take over here until the parents get home."

"Really?" Sage said, with a level of enthusiasm that was way more appropriate for, say, stumbling upon one's own surprise party than it was for hanging out with Martin.

"Of course!" said Malia.

"The mall!" said Martin again.

"You guys have fun at the mall," said Malia, quickly ushering them off before Martin could speak again and potentially ruin her perfect plan. Still, given Sage's expression, she had a feeling he could say virtually anything and it wouldn't matter. "Enjoy the tour! Play some games! Eat some cheese fries for me!"

Sage waved at Malia, mouthing *thank you* behind Martin's back.

No, thank YOU, Malia thought, closing the door behind her.

She breathed a sigh of relief. She heard the familiar sound of the Gregory children laughing in the living room. She felt the presence of Connor—*her* Connor, sort of—somewhere in the house next door. It may have been one small step, but Malia knew that soon enough, everything would be back to how it should be.

"Mawia! Wheya have you been?" asked Jonah, appearing from the living room. He made a beeline for Malia's leg, which he promptly attached himself to.

"I was just taking care of some business!" Malia said. "And now I'm here to hang out with you!"

"Yayyyyyy," said Jonah.

"MALIA!" shouted Plum, running into the room. "We missed you!"

"I missed you, too!" said Malia. "I can't wait to hear what you've been up to."

"Mawia! I want to show you my dwawings," said Jonah. "I made a pitcha of you!"

"You drew a picture of me?" said Malia. She thought she felt her heart melting, just a little bit.

"He did," said Plum. "It's actually pretty good. You're wearing a striped shirt and everything."

"Wow! I'm flattered! And I can't wait to see it." Yep. Definitely heart melt.

"You should hang out fowevah," said Jonah.

"Okay," said Malia. "That sounds like a plan."

CHAPTER THIRTY-FOUR

Bree

"I know you hate me, but I'm still sad," said Bree.

Veronica said nothing.

Bree had tried her very best, but her mom had finally had enough. The curtains were shredded to smithereens, the planters had all been compromised, and the piano would never sound the same. Despite many very passionate protests on Bree's part, today was the day Veronica went back to the cat café.

Bree had tried to make Veronica happy, but she had only failed. Veronica had been telling her all along, in cat language, that this was not the right home for him, and Bree was not his person. She knew it was wrong to keep him in a place that made him so unhappy, and she had accepted that it was time to let him go. She could only hope that he would find his way to the right home.

"Veronica, I thought we could do better." Bree sighed. "Life isn't going to be the same without you."

Still, Veronica said nothing.

Bree picked up a silver sequined pillow from the floor and placed it back on the bed. The sequins sparkled a bit in the sunlight, making tiny glimmers of light dance on the bedroom walls. At the sight of the pillow, Veronica's eyes flashed. Just as quickly, he was airborne, claws swatting at the air.

"Hey . . . wait a second." Bree suddenly had a thought. Not just any thought—a thought that could save everything. *Could it be?*

She decided to conduct a little experiment. Bree picked up the pillow and held it up so it caught the light. She turned it slowly from side to side, allowing the silver sequins to sparkle in the sun. Just as she suspected, Veronica reacted furiously, meowing and hissing and violently clawing at the carpet. "I see," said Bree as she buried the pillow safely underneath her comforter. "It's gone," she said.

Just as dramatically, Veronica calmed down. He plopped down on the rug and started licking his foot as though nothing had ever happened. Bree couldn't believe she didn't see it before.

"You hate glitter," she said.

"Meow," said Veronica. Bree couldn't be sure, but for a split second, it looked like he may have smiled.

Suddenly, everything was crystal clear. Veronica hated glitter. Glitter was Bree's favorite color. Everything in her room was glittery, and she was almost always covered in it. Glitter purses, glitter nail polish, glitter eye shadow, glitter leggings . . . almost everything Bree owned was doused in some kind of sparkles. She even had a glittery garbage can.

Bree thought back to the times she had tried to dress Veronica in glittery outfits, and the few times she had even succeeded. She thought of the glittery mice and his complete refusal to play with them. She thought of all the glittery objects covering every inch of her room and how often they would catch the light. Those were the moments he'd behaved like an absolute psychopath. But when Bree was dressed in plain clothes, like after school when Brody came over, Veronica acted fine.

"MOM! COME QUICK!" Bree yelled.

"Yes?" Her mom appeared at the doorway, panicked.

"I figured it out!" Bree shouted. "Veronica hates glitter!"

"What? What are you talking about?" asked her mom.

"I did an experiment, and I know why he acts out! Shiny things make him go nuts."

Bree's mom crossed her arms. "Are you sure you're not just saying this because you don't want to return him?"

"No! Look."

Bree demonstrated, this time taking a bejeweled hoodie out of her closet and holding it up in the air. At the sight of sparkles, Veronica arched his back and started to hiss. Bree approached him, holding the hoodie out in front of her.

Veronica let out a deranged screech and proceeded to scramble up the already-shredded curtains. Safely out of the glitter's way, he perched on top of the curtain rod, scowling.

"Okay, okay! I believe you," said Bree's mom. "What a special animal."

Bree put the hoodie back in her closet and closed the door. Veronica waited a moment to be sure the coast was clear, then slowly made his way down the curtains.

"Meow," he said, and curled up near Bree's feet.

"Look! He's basically a regular cat!" Bree exclaimed. "He just hates glitter!"

"Meow," said Veronica in agreement.

"So can we keep him?" she pleaded. "Please? Can we try one more time, to see if he behaves without any glitter around?"

Bree's mom thought for a moment. "If this glitter business

really is true, you'll have to make some pretty big changes around here."

Bree sighed. Her mom was right. Glitter was her greatest love, besides cats. If this was ever going to work, she would have to change her entire lifestyle. New room, new wardrobe, new look. "A life without sparkles," she whispered. It sounded so plain.

"Meow!" said Veronica, looking up at her with his big yellow eyes.

Veronica was like her baby. Her very needy, very misunderstood baby. When she signed up for pet parenthood, she didn't expect it to be anything like this. For starters, she thought it would be more fun. Bree had expected to feed him and to bathe him and, sure, to clean the litter box from time to time. She expected it to be work. She didn't expect it to include sacrifice.

Bree glanced around her room, taking a mental tally of all the glittery things she would have to say goodbye to. Was this what growing up felt like? Painful and confusing and utterly impossible? Bree feared the answer was yes.

"Meow?" Veronica blinked.

"I know," Bree said. "Life is confusing."

Bree reasoned she could still visit glitter at the mall. She could still decorate with glitter in her locker at school. Most importantly, the spirit of glitter could live on forever, in her heart.

"All right," said Bree, firm in her decision. "No more glitter."

She hoped it was worth it.

For the second time maybe ever, Veronica purred.

CHAPTER THIRTY-FIVE

Dot

Dot placed exactly five drops of the formula in the test tube and waited. Within seconds, it began to fizz. She recorded her observations, satisfied with its progress. Since the fair was over, she was amazed at how relaxing her actual science class had become (although not everyone shared the sentiment).

At the next table over, Pigeon sat working on the same experiment, but in her case it wasn't going as swimmingly. She seemed dejected. She sat with her shoulders hunched, her head hanging low. She stopped between every step to stare listlessly around the room. Not even the sequin denim jacket she was wearing in place of a lab coat could make the situation look any better.

She couldn't believe it, but Dot actually felt kind of bad for her. The situation reminded her of one of her mom's favorite sayings: "Be kind, for everyone you meet is fighting a hard battle."

Dot reluctantly realized that "everyone" also included Pigeon.

After Pigeon had been disqualified, Dot had been awarded the grand prize, chilly bees and all. So the world had a sense of justice, after all. Pigeon had brought this on herself the moment she had chosen to lie. Still, it was also a terrible way to start off one's seventh-grade career, especially at a new school. Pigeon had already made a reputation for herself, and Dot couldn't imagine how embarrassing that must feel.

After lab, Dot was cleaning up her station when she sensed someone standing over her.

"Hey," came Pigeon's gravelly voice.

Dot reluctantly glanced up. Just because she felt sympathy for Pigeon didn't mean she wanted to talk to her. She hadn't only cheated the system; she had taken advantage of a five-year-old child. She could still recall Aloysius's anger and disappointment when he discovered what had happened.

"I'm sorry for what went down with the science fair. I wasn't thinking straight. I didn't even realize I was cheating, really. I just wanted to have a great project so everyone would be impressed."

"Okay," Dot said flatly.

Maybe Pigeon wasn't a bad person. Maybe she was just a middle school student who recently moved away from the only home she had ever known and was navigating a place where she didn't know anyone and they didn't know her. Dot thought about how the last few weeks had been for her, feeling displaced by the presence of just one new person. How hard must it be to have *everything* around you be new? And to have to show everyone what you're all about?

Pigeon may have been a lying liar-face, but she was still a human being. Human beings made mistakes. And maybe Dot owed her just one more chance.

"All right," said Dot finally. "Consider it a clean slate." Dot was willing to try. Maybe, with time, she could learn to tolerate or maybe even enjoy Pigeon's presence.

"Thank you," said Pigeon, extending her hand. "Also, congratulations on your win. It was well deserved."

Dot tentatively reached out and shook Pigeon's hand.

"Thanks," she said, cracking a small smile.

For once, Pigeon was right.

"This is better," Aloysius said. "This is so much better."

All three original sitters had gathered to watch Aloysius after school. They were so excited to be back babysitting, they'd decided to make it a group endeavor.

Bree raided her family's cabinets and brought a backpack stuffed with her own weight in snacks. They'd spread everything out all over the floor, and were taking the time to catch up on everything they'd missed in the last few weeks. It felt more like a party than a paying job.

"So, where did you put your trophy?" he asked.

"On my bookshelf," Dot said.

"If you want an extra set of hands leading up to the county science fair, I'm happy to help," he said. "It wouldn't count as cheating! The work would be all yours. I could be your apprentice."

"I appreciate that, and I might take you up on it."

Dot's plan was to revamp the hive coolant device over the course of the coming weeks, and an apprentice would be very helpful. Now that she was back to babysitting, time with Aloysius was a given.

"How's Veronica?" Aloysius asked.

"Like a whole new cat," Bree said, munching on cheddar popcorn. "I also have a whole new wardrobe, but I'm starting to get used to it."

"You can find new ways to express yourself now," said Dot.

In the absence of glitter, Bree had taken to wearing bright colors. Today she wore neon pink jeans and a neon pink shirt.

"Yeah," Bree conceded. "Veronica is worth it. I'm so in love with his wrinkly face."

"I understand what it means to fall in love with a face." Malia sighed.

"We know you do," said Dot.

"Speaking of love," said Bree. "Would it be totally cheesy to say that I love being here? And that I love all of you?"

"Yes, it would be totally cheesy," said Dot.

"But seriously, I'm proud of us," said Malia. "We hired the satellite sitters because we wanted growth. And maybe it wasn't the kind of growth we were after, but I think we've all made a bunch of personal progress lately, wouldn't you say?"

"Yes," said Dot.

"I agree, but now can we stop growing for a minute?" said Bree. "I'm tired."

"I'm exhausted," said Malia.

"Dr. Puffin says sometimes the best thing you can do is to stand still to really appreciate the moment."

"Stillness," said Aloysius, thinking. "You know, Einstein said, 'I think ninety-nine times and find nothing. I stop thinking, swim in stillness, and the answer comes to me.'"

"Deep," said Malia.

Dot looked around the room, doing her best to appreciate the moment. Seeing her best friends and the amazing little boy before her, she realized, in that moment, she had everything she had ever wanted.

CHAPTER THIRTY-SIX

MALIA

Malia was once told that success happens when opportunity meets preparation. (She was offered this gem by Ramona, who at the time was trying to make a point about how Malia hadn't prepared properly for connecting a conference call with a Supreme Court justice.) As with most things in Malia's world, whenever she looked back on this advice, she wondered how she could apply it to the most elusive of enterprises: Connor.

Preparation + Opportunity = Success.

Malia had certainly prepared. She observed him. She researched his favorite things. She imagined their conversations. She'd attended a concert for him. She even tried to practice the manifesting techniques Dot's mom was always talking about. It was quite possible that Malia had never been more prepared for anything. But that was only one side of success. She was still waiting on opportunity.

Finally, on one random Tuesday afternoon, opportunity came knocking.

Malia was going for a walk when she decided to wander past the Gregory house—okay fine, she was walking by Connor's house. Whatever. As always, she slowed down as she approached the block, just in case he was in the vicinity.

"Heads up!" yelled a voice. *The* voice. Malia knew that voice anywhere. She was *prepared* for that voice.

She turned to see not only the glorious face that the voice came out of, but also a soccer ball, sailing in her direction. She didn't have time to think. She barely had time to react. So she did what any self-respecting person (with somewhat decent eye-hand coordination) would do: she kicked the ball back. And then—OH MY GOD WHAT WAS HAPPENING— Connor kicked the ball back to her.

It went on this way for what felt like an eternity but was actually three and a half minutes. They might have been the most beautiful three and a half minutes of Malia's life.

"You're pretty good at passing," Connor said.

They were the nicest words Malia had ever heard.

"Thanks," she said.

"Sure," said Connor.

"Do you want to, like, play a game on purpose sometime?" Malia asked. "Like at Marvelous Ray's or something?" She had no idea where the words were coming from. Had she just *asked Connor Kelly on a sort of, maybe date?*

"Yeah! That sounds great," said Connor.

HE SAID YES.

Just then, Aidan Morrison appeared near the side of the yard.

Go away, Aidan, thought Malia. But he didn't go away. Instead he made noise, the way boys so often do.

"Connor!" he called. "Are you coming?"

"Yeah!" Connor yelled back. "Bye, Malia," he said with a small wave, as he started to dribble away.

Once again, Malia found herself in a very familiar position: staring at Connor's back. But this time, she was also full of hope that maybe, just maybe, this was a step in the right direction.

"Isn't it amazing that we're, you know, alive?" Malia asked. She gazed up at the gazebo's ceiling, thinking about everything that had happened there.

"What are you talking about?" Dot asked.

"Sometimes I look around, at the sky and the flowers and the trees, and I'm like, what a marvelous world we live in." Malia sighed.

Dot looked concerned. "Are you on some kind of controlled substance? Do I need to be worried?"

"Connor kicked a soccer ball at her. And then he talked to her," Bree said.

"Ohhh," Dot said, suddenly understanding.

"He didn't kick it *at* me, he kicked it *to* me," Malia said. After all, it was a very important distinction. "Then we kicked it back and forth. For, like, a long time."

"I see. Sounds dreamy." Dot rolled her eyes.

"Just because he's not your type doesn't mean you can't be happy for me," Malia huffed.

"Obviously I am happy for you. And if you and Connor ever have an actual conversation where, say, fifteen or more words are exchanged, I will be even happier."

"YOU AND ME BOTH," Malia said.

She was brought back down to earth by the sound of her phone. It was probably Ramona, asking for goodness knows what. But instead of Ramona's name, she saw a number she didn't recognize.

"Hello, I'm looking for a babysitter. Can you help me?" a woman's voice came through the line.

"Yes," said Malia, putting her phone on speaker so her friends could be involved.

"I need to hire some after-school help for my daughter," said the woman. She sounded a bit desperate.

"Of course!" said Malia.

"And if it goes well, maybe you could even go to some activities with her. The movies, the mall, a sports event, you know, that kind of thing."

"That all sounds great. How often would you like someone to be there?"

"On a verrrrrrry regular basis," said the woman. "I'd say most weekdays, after school."

"Wow," said Malia.

That was a pretty big commitment. It was also a lot of money.

"Depending on how it goes, we may be interested in finding some time on the weekends."

"Okay, then! Let's find a time for us to come and meet your daughter and we'll see what we can do."

Malia scheduled a meet and greet for later that week.

"Every single day? That sounds weird," said Dot.

"Maybe, but do you know how much money that is? We can take turns so we still have time for other jobs," Malia said. "This could be huge."

"I guess it can't hurt to try it!" said Bree, ever the optimist.

"I never thought I'd say this, but I am so glad to be back to babysitting," said Dot.

"Me too," said Malia.

"Me three," said Bree.

"Like I was saying. Isn't it amazing we're alive?" said Malia. Her Connor high had been met by a new-business high. Now she was pretty much in love with everything.

"Yeah," said Dot as a bee buzzed by. "It actually kind of is amazing."

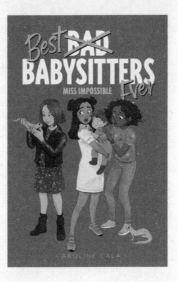

The Best Babysitters are psyched to land their highest paying job yet—until they get to the house and realize they're babysitting Zelda Hooper, the meanest girl in school. And even though Zelda should be the one who's embarrassed that three girls her age are babysitting her, she finds ways to thwart them at every turn.

But Zelda isn't the girls' only challenge. A new crop of French au pairs are stealing all their business—*Quelle catastrophe!*—forcing Dot to watch the rambunctious Morris boys, whose idea of a good time is lighting things on fire, while Bree teams up with Malia's pushy older sister to tackle a new pet cause: saving the salamanders of Playa del Mar.

Will Malia, Dot, and Bree be able to handle their impossible new charges—or will this be the end of the Best Babysitters forever?